MIGHTY MORPHIN
POWER RANGERS

MAYHEM FROM MOON PALACE

by Alexander Irvine

Penguin Young Readers Licenses
An Imprint of Penguin Random House

PENGUIN YOUNG READERS LICENSES
An Imprint of Penguin Random House LLC

Cover illustration by Dan Panosian

ISBN 9781524783815   10 9 8 7 6 5 4 3 2 1

Chapter 1

Bright and early on a Saturday morning in May, four of the six teenagers who make up the Mighty Morphin Power Rangers waited in the Angel Grove High School parking lot. Jason Scott leaned casually against his car, next to his best friend, Zack Taylor. Around school, they both were known mostly as athletes, but Zack was a practical joker, too. Jason had a more thoughtful side, teaching martial arts and going out of his way to be kind and responsible. On either side of them were Kimberly Hart and Tommy Oliver. Kimberly was a gymnast, dancer, and musician, while Tommy—the newest member of the group, and a bit of an outsider in school—shared Jason and Zack's interest in martial arts.

They were waiting for Billy Cranston and Trini Kwan to show up with their experiment for the district science fair. It was mostly Billy's idea, from what they understood, but Trini had pitched in, too. Sometimes she was the only other Power Ranger who could understand what Billy was talking about when he got talking about science.

Jason had parked all the way across the lot, past the football stadium, because Billy didn't want anyone to see his experiment before he unveiled it in the gym. So they were all supposed to meet there and carry it in under a sheet.

Billy was being super secretive about the whole thing. Over the past few weeks, he hadn't even told them what the experiment was. Now they were all dying to see it.

Billy's customized Beetle, the Rad Bug, came rolling toward them from around the back of the stadium. He parked next to Jason's car and got out, looking around to see if anyone was watching. There were no cars within a hundred yards. "You didn't fly?" Jason joked. "Would have gotten you here a lot quicker." The Rad Bug had a ton of modifications, including the ability to fly and remote-control operation.

"No way," Billy said. "I wish I had a way to make it invisible." He opened the trunk. Inside sat a big square object wrapped in a sheet. "Trini and I made a little platform to help carry it," Billy said. "Zack, give me a hand."

The two of them picked it up. "Man, this thing weighs a ton," Zack said. He eyed the distance to the school.

"We can carry it in shifts," Tommy said. "You guys start. Halfway there, Jason and I will take over."

"That lets me and Kimberly off the hook," Trini said.

"You had to help him already this morning," Zack said. "You've done your part."

"What's that supposed to mean?" Billy asked.

"You've been kind of tense about this lately, Billy," Trini said. "In case you haven't noticed."

"I have not been tense!" Billy said. "Have I?"

Kimberly patted him on the shoulder. "Maybe a little."

"Well, it's a big deal. If I win, I go on to the state finals."

"You'll win," Tommy said. "There's nobody smarter than you."

"We'll see," Billy said.

At the edge of the lot, on the access road that curved around the back of the stadium, there was a maintenance shed. It held a couple of lawn mowers and the machine used to paint the lines on the football field. Jason happened to be looking that way over Zack's shoulder, and he saw something move. At first he thought it was an animal.

No, two animals.

Wait, three . . . and they weren't animals, at all. They were Putties!

"Guys," Jason said. "You might want to put the experiment down."

Zack looked over his shoulder to see what Jason saw, but he couldn't turn far enough and still hold the experiment. He started to lower it. "Not on the ground!" Billy yelled. They put it back in the trunk.

"Putties?" Trini was already dropping into a fighting stance. "What are they doing here?"

"Maybe Lord Zedd doesn't want Billy to win the science fair," Zack joked.

Billy didn't smile. "That's really not funny."

"Better morph, guys," Jason said. He took a quick look around the lot. Everyone else coming to the fair was parked around the other side of the school, closer to the door. "Okay. It's Morphin Time!"

Chapter 2

They called out their team signals in sequence: "Dragonzord!" "Mastodon!" "Pterodactyl!" "Triceratops!" "Sabertooth Tiger!" "Tyrannosaurus!"

As each one spoke, they morphed and became Power Rangers. Jason became the Red Ranger, Zack the Black Ranger, Trini the Yellow Ranger, Billy the Blue Ranger, Kimberly the Pink Ranger, and Tommy the Green Ranger. They joined forces to battle the Putties.

These weren't the old Putties that Rita Repulsa used to send after them. Lord Zedd had his own Z-Putties, stronger and smarter than Rita's. Lord Zedd marked each with his signature Z on their chest plates, but those plates were also their weakness. A strong blow right on the Z would blow a Z-Putty apart. The problem was getting a shot at the Z. The Z-Putties didn't make it easy. They would be a handful, even though there were only three of them.

In a flash of light, two more forms appeared on top of the shed: Rita's minions Baboo and Squatt! Baboo squinted at the Power Rangers through his monocle. Like Squatt, he had blue skin, but there the resemblance ended. Baboo was tall and thin, bat-like in appearance and dressed all in black. Squatt looked much like a blue warthog on two legs, in metal armor with heavy fangs jutting up from his lower jaw.

"What have you got there, Rangers?" they called out. "We'll take it!"

The Blue Ranger stepped out in front of the group. "Oh no, you won't."

The rest flanked him and faced the Z-Putties. More had appeared after the first three. Now there were six, spreading out in a half circle. The Green and Pink Rangers charged out to stop the Z-Putties from surrounding the team. The Black and Yellow Rangers teamed up to cut off one of the Z-Putties from the group. They knocked it down but couldn't get a clear shot at its Z. Billy and Kimberly tried the same with another Z-Putty, but they found themselves fighting off three Z-Putties at once. Tommy came flying in and knocked down one of the Z-Putties, giving Kimberly and Billy some breathing room.

Jason figured the other Power Rangers could handle the Z-Putties for a minute. "You guys keep at it. I'm headed after Baboo and Squatt!" he called out, running toward the shed and jumping to catch the edge of its roof. As he pulled himself up, Baboo and Squatt squealed in fear and tumbled off the other side of the roof. They bounced through the brush behind the shed and ran away. Jason would have gone after them, but there were still Z-Putties to deal with . . . and as he turned to do that, there was a shimmer of light at the edge of the parking lot, and Goldar appeared.

"Look out!" Jason called. "Goldar!"

Baboo and Squatt never fought. All they did was talk a lot and then run away. But Goldar was a different story. Huge and apelike, with black wings, he wore golden armor and wielded a long golden sword. He had always wanted to destroy the Power Rangers to please Rita Repulsa, but now that Lord Zedd had taken over and banished Rita, Goldar was loyal to him. He was eager to please his new master.

Goldar raised his sword and pointed it at Jason.

"Lord Zedd commands you to surrender or be destroyed!"

"We'll take option three," Jason called back.

"What? I only gave you two options!"

"Option three is sending you back to Lord Zedd with a message," Jason said. "The Power Rangers will never surrender to him!"

He jumped and somersaulted off the shed roof, landing near Goldar and dropping into a fighting stance.

Goldar stepped up to meet him as one of the Z-Putties flew to pieces nearby. Tommy had hit it square in the Z with a palm heel. The team had a good handle on the Z-Putties. That gave Tommy a chance to go after Goldar.

"Oh, I've been waiting for this!" he said.

He and Goldar had a history. Goldar had never yet defeated him in single combat, and Tommy was always ready to extend his winning streak. He charged straight at Goldar, who barely had time to get his sword up before Tommy got him with a flying kick. Goldar staggered back, flaring his wings for balance. Jason leaped forward, hitting Goldar again before he could recover.

The other Power Rangers were starting to turn the tide against the Z-Putties. Tommy had destroyed one. Now Kimberly ducked under a Z-Putty's spinning kick. She popped back up and put everything she had into a reverse elbow to its chest plate. The point of her elbow hit the engraved Z dead center, and the Z-Putty reeled back. A moment later, it blew apart into bits of clay.

Billy and Trini sparred with another Z-Putty, waiting for it to give them an opening. When it turned a little too far trying to spin away from Billy's kick, Trini saw her chance. She shot out a kick and planted her heel in the Z. The Z-Putty blew apart.

There were only three Z Putties left now. Jason and Tommy kept after Goldar, not letting him fight either alone.

"I got this," Jason said. "You help with the Z-Putties."

"You sure?" Tommy glanced back at the Z-Putties. "Goldar knows he can't beat us if we face him together."

"Yes, I can!" Goldar roared. With a quick swipe, he knocked Tommy flat on his back with a blow from his sword.

Jason jumped in before Goldar could hit Tommy again. He blocked Goldar's sword and punched him three times in the head, stunning him. Tommy jumped up and joined in, pounding Goldar with a flying kick. Then he dashed back to rejoin the rest of the team against the Z-Putties.

Kimberly and Trini had just taken out another Z-Putty. Now there were five Power Rangers against only two Z-Putties. Trini knocked one down, and Zack came flying through the air to land on its Z plate with both feet. Pieces of the Z-Putty scattered across the parking lot. Then they all tag-teamed the last one, with Kimberly landing the final punch to its plate.

As the last pieces of the Z-Putty flew through the air and disappeared, the Rangers turned to help Jason against Goldar. Jason was getting back to his feet after Goldar knocked him over, and Tommy led the way, dodging the sweep of Goldar's massive sword.

"Come on, Power Rangers," Jason said. "Let's deliver that message."

They formed a circle around Goldar and came closer. Goldar turned around, trying to keep them all in front of him. Then he flared his wings and said, "You have not defeated me, Power Rangers! I will be back!"

In a flash of light, Goldar was gone. The Power Rangers were alone in the parking lot again.

Chapter 3

From his throne room in the Moon Palace he now ruled, Lord Zedd watched the battle unfold. The throne room's lights shone on his armor and his skinless body. His disfigured face was hidden behind the black-and-silver helmet he always wore, with a letter Z as its crest, but his tone of voice left no doubt about his mood.

"Soon these Power Rangers will learn what it truly means to oppose me!" he growled. "I will find their weakness once and for all, and I will destroy them!"

Baboo and Squatt appeared in the throne room a moment later.

"Useless idiots!" Zedd roared. He pointed a clawed finger at them. "You were supposed to distract the Red Ranger and keep him apart from the others so Goldar could attack him!"

"We tried, Lord Zedd," Baboo said. "We did

everything and gave it our all."

"Gave it your all? From the top of the shed? Fools, do you forget that I am always watching? I see how useless you are, cowards! Get out of my sight before I banish you!"

Goldar transported in as Baboo and Squatt fled. Zedd waited until he was sure they were gone. He wanted to speak only to Goldar, and often Baboo and Squatt hid behind a wall in the throne room, watching and listening. But this time they had run away to another part of the base. *Good*, Zedd thought. He would deal with them later.

"Goldar, of all Rita's minions, I thought you were worth keeping," he said.

"If you say so, it must be true, Lord Zedd," Goldar said. "You are always right."

"But you could not defeat them, even with my most powerful Z-Putties to assist you!" Zedd clenched a fist. "You had the Red Ranger cut off, and you let his friends help him! How could you let that happen? Perhaps I was wrong about you. Perhaps you belong in a space Dumpster like that old space witch Rita Repulsa."

"No, Lord Zedd!" Goldar cried out. "I will do

exactly what you command and destroy the Power Rangers next time. The Red Ranger will not be able to defeat me again."

"See that he doesn't," Zedd said. "I have given you too many chances already."

Chapter 4

Fearful of what Lord Zedd would do if he found them, Baboo and Squatt went all the way to Finster's laboratory, where he created bizarre creatures and strange machines. He was a small gray creature, bearded with long, pointed ears, and he was much more at home in his laboratory than anywhere else. He hadn't come out since Lord Zedd had banished Rita because he was afraid Lord Zedd would banish him, too.

"What are you two doing here?" he snapped, glaring at Baboo and Squatt as they entered.

"We are hiding from Lord Zedd!" Squatt shut the door behind them and leaned against it. "He threatened to banish us."

"He blames us for everything," Baboo added.

"Well, soon he will change his mind." Finster placed a circuit carefully in a nest of wires. He linked them all together.

"How? What are you doing there?" Squatt came too close to Finster's project, and Finster leaned over to block his view.

"I can't tell you," he said. "I am working."

"On what?" Baboo asked. He looked closely at what Finster was doing.

"I'll tell you when it's ready," Finster said.

"Tell us now!" Squatt begged.

Finster considered. On the one hand, he was afraid of being banished, and he could use some allies. Lord Zedd might not banish them all at once, if they stuck together. On the other hand, if he told Baboo and Squatt too much, they might tell Lord Zedd.

Finster didn't want Zedd to know what he was doing. He wanted it to be a surprise—one that would prove Finster's worth to Lord Zedd. That would keep him out of a space Dumpster like the one where Rita Repulsa was currently sitting, somewhere out in orbit.

So he didn't really want to tell them anything. The problem was that Finster knew Baboo and Squatt too well to think they would keep a secret.

If he told them nothing, though . . . they would tell Lord Zedd he was working on something the minute he did anything to scare them. And then Finster would have to face Lord Zedd. He wouldn't have any help from Baboo and Squatt. They would do anything to keep Lord Zedd's fearsome temper pointed away from them.

Finster decided the best thing to do was tell them part of what he was doing. That would keep them happy for the moment.

"Fine," he said. "I am building a device that will take control of Zordon's irritating robot, Alpha 5. But you can't tell Lord Zedd because it is supposed to be a secret."

"Oh, I don't know if we should keep secrets from Lord Zedd," Squatt said. He started to tremble at the thought.

"Don't think of it as a secret. Think of it as a surprise."

That seemed to make Squatt feel better. Finster explained more. "Remember, Lord Zedd thinks we are all useless because Rita could not destroy the Power Rangers. We have to prove ourselves, yes?"

Baboo and Squatt both nodded.

"That's what this machine will do. I will finish it, and Alpha 5 will be mine to control! I will force him to deactivate the Thunderzords, and then the Power Rangers will have to face Lord Zedd on their own. He will defeat them, and we will look good because we helped!" Finster waited for this to sink in. Then he added, "But it will only work if you keep quiet until I am done."

"We will," Baboo said.

"And steer clear of Lord Zedd. Do not give him any reason to be angry at you."

"Oh no, we won't," Squatt promised.

"Good," Finster said. "Now go hide somewhere else. I have work to do."

Chapter 5

The Power Rangers morphed back into their regular clothes and looked around the parking lot. There was no trace of the Z-Putties, and no one near the school had noticed. Students from all over the Angel Grove area were bringing in their experiments. "It's almost time for the fair to start," Billy said. "We'd better get inside. I need a few minutes to get everything set up."

Jason nodded. "Okay. I'll stay here, talk to Zordon, and make sure no more Z-Putties are coming. You guys go on in and help Billy set up."

"Got it." Zack hefted his end of Billy's experiment. "Come on, Billy."

Jason held up his wrist-communicator as the rest of the Rangers walked away toward the school. "Zordon," he said. "We're at the school for the science fair, but we also battled Goldar and a squad of Z-Putties."

"Yes! We were just about to check in," Zordon answered. "Is everyone all right?"

"Aye-yi-yi," Alpha 5 said. "Why did Goldar run away?"

"I was wondering about that, too," Jason said. "Usually he puts up more of a fight."

"Lord Zedd is planning something," Zordon said. "I am watching him, but I don't know exactly what his plan is just yet. You must be prepared for him to attack again."

"We will be," Jason promised.

"I have scanned the area," Zordon said, "but I don't see anything out of the ordinary. Perhaps you should search to be sure."

"Okay," Jason said. "I'll take a look."

"Report back the moment you see anything," Zordon said. "And tell Billy we're wishing him the best in the science competition!"

"I will." Jason looked around the area. Behind the shed and the football stadium, low hills rose. There weren't many houses out that way. A few miles into the hills was the secret location of Zordon's Command Center.

Jason decided to start with the area right around the school. He passed the shed and climbed the closest hill to get a better view. When he got to the top, he didn't see anything, but Zordon was right. Lord Zedd could have created some kind of monster. He'd done it before. It could be anywhere, waiting for Lord Zedd to order it to attack.

But if he couldn't see it, he couldn't fight it. Zordon would know if there was an active threat. Jason turned to head for the gym. He wanted to be there to support Billy.

Chapter 6

Inside the Angel Grove High School gym, dozens of students were setting up their experiments. Each had an assigned booth. There were four double rows of booths, stretching the whole length of the gym. The judges' table was at the far end, near the door to the girls' locker room.

Zack and Tommy set down Billy's experiment at his booth. There was a folding table, an easel, and two chairs, with space for displays on either side. Many of the teams had set up posters to explain what they were doing. "Let's get it up on the table," Billy said.

When they had it centered on the table, Billy carefully lifted the sheet away and folded it. "Man," Tommy said. "I don't know what that thing is, but it sure looks cool."

Billy beamed. His experiment looked kind of like a computer and kind of like an airplane control panel. It had several screens, knobs and dials, and two antennas that Billy extended and arranged so they pointed up and out at an angle.

"What does it do?" Zack asked.

Billy was about to answer, but then he looked around and said, "Oh, I forgot. I left my posters in my car!"

"I'll get them," Kimberly said. "Don't explain until I get back."

She jogged through the crowd and out of the gym. As she crossed the parking lot toward Billy's car, she looked around for Jason. He wasn't anywhere in sight. She thought about calling him, but he was probably still standing guard against the Z-Putties. He would be back soon.

The poster boards were in the back seat of Billy's car. She collected them and walked toward the school. It was kind of hard to jog holding poster boards.

When she was almost to the door, her wrist-communicator chirped. When she answered, Zordon said, "Rangers! The Morphin Grid has detected a threat somewhere inside the school. I am not certain what it is, but you must search the whole building immediately!"

Uh-oh, Kimberly thought. She started running, holding the poster board awkwardly out in front of her.

She got to Billy's booth and saw that the rest of the team had heard Zordon's call. They looked nervous because they couldn't answer inside the gym. No one could know the secret of the Power Rangers. Quickly Kimberly filled them in.

"We're going to have to split up and search the school," Trini said.

"Let's go," Zack said.

Kimberly looked back toward the door. "Without Jason?"

"He would have heard Zordon just like we did," Trini pointed out. "He'll be here."

"Unless . . ." Billy hesitated as they all looked at him.

"Unless what?" Tommy prompted him.

"Unless he can't get back," Billy said.

They looked at one another for a long, nervous moment. Then Tommy said, "Jason can take care of himself. We should follow Zordon's orders. Let's get looking."

"Okay," Billy said. "But the fair's about to start. Let's move fast."

They headed out as a group, splitting up when they got to the gym doors. Trini and Billy went left, toward the auditorium and the swimming pool. The other three headed for the classroom wings. They all were worried about Jason, but they had to trust Zordon.

Chapter 7

Jason heard Zordon's warning and started running. He was at the edge of the stadium, and he made it back to the shed at the far end of the parking lot quickly. He was raising his wrist-communicator to ask the rest of the Power Rangers where he should meet them, when suddenly he skidded to a halt.

Goldar was there, next to Jason's car. Good thing they'd parked way out there, far from any other cars or people. "You are alone, Red Ranger! Right where I want you!"

Waiting for him.

"Tyrannosaurus!" Jason called out. He felt the flash of energy around him as the power of the Morphin Grid changed him from ordinary Angel Grove teenager Jason Scott to the Red Power Ranger, defender of Earth. Flushed with the feeling of power, he stepped toward Goldar.

"You're between me and my friends," he said.

"That is not a good place to be."

Goldar raised his sword and spread his wings as Jason came at him. He rang a punch off Goldar's armor and followed it with a kick to Goldar's midsection. But Goldar recovered quickly, and Jason barely dodged back in time to avoid a wild swing from Goldar's sword. Then he had to keep backpedaling as Goldar kept swinging.

"Lord Zedd will rule this world, Power Ranger! I fight for him!"

Tell me something I don't know, Jason thought. He ducked behind a car, and Goldar smashed his sword down on its hood. The car's front tires blew out.

Jason came around the back of the car and launched a spinning split kick into Goldar's back. He squared up, and as Goldar turned around, Jason caught him with a chop to the side of the neck. Goldar roared and flapped his massive wings forward. They slapped Jason in the face. His Power Ranger helmet protected him, but the impact still sent him flying backward.

Jason reached out and caught one of Goldar's wings, flinging him aside into the wrecked car. He wanted to call the other Power Rangers, but if they were still inside the school, someone would hear. He couldn't take the chance. That meant he was on his own.

"Zordon!" he called out, through the helmet comm link. "Goldar is in the school parking lot!"

"I see you, Red Ranger," came Zordon's voice.

In the background, Jason could hear Alpha 5 fretting. "Aye-yi-yi, Jason should have the rest of the Power Rangers with him!"

"You must keep Goldar from getting to the school," Zordon warned.

"I don't think he wants to." Jason dodged back as Goldar rushed at him again. "He seems pretty focused on me."

"Then Lord Zedd must have sent him after you specifically," Zordon said. "He might have another plan to attack the rest of the Rangers. I will warn them."

"It might take them a minute to answer. They're in the school with a lot of people around," Jason said. Then he was too busy to talk because Goldar was hacking at him with the sword again. He ducked and parried by striking at Goldar's arms to deflect his sword strokes.

But Goldar was strong. If they weren't so close to the school, Jason would have kept trying to handle

Goldar on his own, but Zordon was right. He couldn't risk someone at the school getting hurt.

Then Lord Zedd upped the stakes. One of his grenades fell from the sky and surrounded Goldar in a flash of light. When the light faded, Goldar had grown to his full enormous size, looming over Jason and raising his sword, which was suddenly as long as a bus. At that size, Goldar was a real danger to the school and everyone in it. He had escalated the fight, and Jason had to answer.

It was time to call in his Thunderzord.

Jason raised his arms and called out, "Tyrannosaurus Red Dragon Thunderzord Power!"

A roar echoed over the hills, and Jason disappeared just as Goldar's sword cut through the space where he had been. The sword buried itself in the asphalt parking lot. Goldar pulled it free and looked up into the sky.

The Tyrannosaurus Red Dragon Thunderzord swooped over the hills as Jason piloted it down toward Goldar. As Jason dove at him, Goldar struck at the Thunderzord and crashed his blade against its side. The Thunderzord wrapped its tail around Goldar's legs, and its claws hooked into his armor.

Jason leaned back, and the Thunderzord lifted Goldar off the ground.

"There are rules against fighting on school grounds, Goldar," Jason said.

He carried Goldar over the first ridge of hills and let him fall. Goldar flailed and smashed down into the brush in a canyon, a mile from the school. His sword bounced away among the rocks. For a moment he was stunned, but he got up quickly and looked for his sword as Jason swung around to come after him again. The Thunderzord swept its tail across the earth, raising a storm of dust around Goldar. He wanted to keep Goldar from finding his sword while he figured out what to do next. Should he keep trying to delay Goldar out here? What if the rest of the Power Rangers hadn't talked to Zordon because they were inside the school?

Jason didn't have any more time to think about his options because at that moment, Goldar jumped up out of the dust cloud and grabbed on to the Thunderzord's tail, swinging it down to smash against the canyon wall. The impact caused a colossal rockslide. Boulders fell around Goldar, and some hit him. He staggered back and let go of the Thunderzord.

Jason saw his chance and took it. He switched the Thunderzord to Warrior Mode and spun the warrior's staff in a series of strikes that staggered Goldar. Then Goldar struck back, his sword clashing against the Thunderzord's armor and stopping Jason's attack. Jason braced the Thunderzord against the far canyon wall and launched it toward Goldar, putting all its weight into a flying tackle that crushed Goldar against the other wall of the canyon.

Goldar stumbled and sank to his knees. He dropped his sword and fell over, stunned. Jason waited, but Goldar didn't get up.

"Zordon," he said. "Did you talk to the rest of the team?"

"Communications are difficult," Zordon said. "There has been periodic interference with signals. I am unable to reach them."

"I'm headed that way once I take care of our good friend Goldar," Jason said. "I'll find out what's going on soon enough."

Chapter 8

Tommy, Kimberly, and Zack made a long loop around the classroom wings without seeing anything out of the ordinary. Just shut classroom doors and rows and rows of lockers. Even the janitorial closets were closed up tight, except for one. Its door was wedged open with a mop bucket. They looked into it, but all they saw were big jugs of cleaning fluids and a couple of brooms.

"Zordon wouldn't have sent us out if something wasn't going on," Kimberly said. "What did we miss?"

"Let's go back and look again," Tommy said. They doubled back, passing the computer lab and the math classrooms.

Up ahead were the science classrooms. Light flashed under one of the doors. "There," Zack said. "Did you guys see that?"

Tommy nodded. "Yeah. Let's take a look."

They gathered around the door. Kimberly and

Zack stayed off to one side while Tommy got ready to open the door. "Okay," Zack said. "Go."

Tommy jerked the door open, and all three Rangers crowded through the doorway.

The science lab had long worktables arranged in a grid around the central lab table. There were beakers and burners everywhere. Along one wall was a row of aquariums and terrariums where the students kept small animals to study.

There they saw the source of the flashing light.

One of the small tanks held several earthworms, so students could see their tiny tunnels through its glass walls. They made observations about how the worms ate and how fast they could dig. But this morning, something bizarre was happening in that tank.

A worm was crawling up the side, and it was glowing with bluish energy. "Worms can't crawl up glass, can they?" Tommy wondered.

"I don't think so. That's why there's no lid on that tank, right?" Kimberly asked.

The worm got to the rim of the tank. As it poked its head out, it started to grow—and change. One second it was about five inches long and as thick as a pencil. The next second it suddenly stood on the classroom floor, ten feet tall and as big around as a trash barrel. It sprouted arms and legs that were more like tentacles, ending in flaps instead of hands and feet. Its head changed, growing eyes and a mouth.

"Oh, Power Rangers!" it said in a voice that was like someone trying to gargle a mouthful of mud. "Class is in session!"

Tommy's eyes popped. "And it can talk?"

The three Power Rangers morphed and squared off against the monster, spreading out and waiting to see what it would do. They had seen Lord Zedd do this before. He had the power to take an animal and turn it into an intelligent monster. But . . .

"A worm?" Tommy said. "Seriously? I mean, I can see a piranha or an octopus. But an earthworm?"

"That's Wormazam to you!" the monster sneered.

One of its arms lashed out and stretched all the way across the room to knock Tommy sprawling. He banged into a supply cabinet and bounced back to his feet. Kimberly ran to help him up, blocking another swipe from Wormazam's arm. A slime coating from the monster was smeared across her Ranger suit.

Wormazam rushed toward them, but Zack knocked it off balance with a double-footed flying pile driver. He landed on the lab table and danced out of the way when Wormazam tried to slap his legs out from under him with its tail.

Kimberly and Tommy joined in, ducking away from Wormazam's swiping arms and trying to get close enough to attack.

"We have to keep it in here," Kimberly said. "Who knows what it will do if it gets out?"

"Man, we should take it to the reservoir. Wonder what kind of fish we could catch with a worm that big!" Zack was still making cracks even as he did a backflip off the table to avoid a swipe from Wormazam's tail. Beakers smashed on the floor.

But Wormazam was fast, and even when they did hit it, their blows just seemed to bounce off. Kimberly and Tommy jumped back and joined Zack near the door.

"Punches don't even touch it," Tommy said, panting. "It's like it's made out of rubber."

"Time to take things to another level," Zack said. He raised his hands and said, "Power Axe!"

The Power Axe appeared in his hands.

"Power Bow!" Kimberly said, flexing her arms. Her Power Bow appeared, and she drew it taut. "Come on, Tommy!"

Tommy raised a hand, and the Dragon Dagger appeared in a blaze of energy.

They all struck at once. Tommy's dagger slashed through one of Wormazam's arms. Zack swung his Power Axe low, cutting off one of Wormazam's legs and a long piece of its tail. And an arrow from Kimberly's Power Bow exploded when it hit Wormazam's other arm, blasting it off.

Standing on one leg, Wormazam looked with demented glee at its arms and leg and tail wriggling on the floor of the classroom.

"Ahhhh-ha-ha-ha-ha, Rangers!" it cackled. "You know what happens when a worm gets cut in half, don't you?"

"Uh-oh," Kimberly said.

The four separated pieces of Wormazam twisted around and started to change shape. Within a few seconds, they were no longer just an arm or a tail or a leg . . . They were four new, complete Wormazams wriggling about.

"Hit me again!" Wormazam gargled. "There will

just be more Wormazams!" It was growing back the pieces they had cut off. By the time the little Wormazams were done changing, the big Wormazam had grown back everything it had lost.

"Man, that did not work out like I planned it," Zack said.

Chapter 9

Bulk and Skull got their science-fair project unloaded and set up in five minutes flat. They were going to be rich. Skull had found a mirror at a thrift shop that made a person look skinnier, and they had put it up next to a regular mirror Bulk got out of his garage. They put a scale in front of each mirror. The regular mirror had a scale that gave an accurate weight. Skull had fixed the other one so it read ten pounds lighter. Then they had added a bunch of computers to the display so it looked more . . . well, science-y.

"We're gonna win for sure," Bulk declared. "And then we're gonna be rich. We'll have our own infomercial."

Skull was looking around the gym. "Man, Bulk, did you ever see so many geeks in one place?"

"Not since the last science fair," Bulk said.

"You went to the last science fair?"

"Ha! Me? No way! But where else would there

have been so many geeks?" Bulk gave Skull a shove. "Let's look around."

They walked down one of the aisles, gawking at the experiments on both sides. Kids from all over their part of California were there. One table had a mini garden with some kind of new tomato. Another was covered in different kinds of glass with lights that shone through them to make rainbows.

"Huh," Skull said. "Where are the unicorns?"

They stopped by a table that had a solar-powered battery charger.

"How do they know if it works in here?" Bulk wondered. Then the kid behind the table brought out a solar lamp and turned it on. "Oh. Hey, kid. Will that thing give you a sunburn?"

"Um, yeah, I think it will," the kid said. "But I've never tried."

"Whatever," Bulk said. He caught up with Skull, who was now standing in front of a poster covered with math. There was a computer on the table next to it with different-colored shapes curling around in patterns.

The table next to that one didn't have anyone standing behind it. Bulk looked it over, and something caught his attention. "Hey, Skull. Check this out. Billy Cranston."

"Figures," Skull said. "No way would Billy miss out on a nerd fest like this."

They both looked at Billy's experiment. It was some kind of . . . radio, maybe? A computer? They couldn't tell what it was supposed to do. It had too many screens and buttons for them to figure it out. They looked at the posters lying on the table and tried to read them. It was all super-complicated science stuff.

"What's he talking about?" Skull asked Bulk.

Bulk shrugged. "Nerd stuff, man. How should I know?"

Skull squinted. "Targeted . . . anti-dimensional energy . . . coherence disrupter," he read slowly. "Sounds like he just made that up. I mean, what does that mean?"

Bulk was looking past him. "Hey," he said. "I have an idea."

Skull looked where Bulk was looking. He saw a pair of judges talking to one of the science nerds three tables over.

"What idea?" Skull asked.

Bulk grinned at him. "What if we pass this off as our project?"

"What? How are we gonna do that, Bulk? We can barely read this stuff!"

"Seriously," Bulk said. "We hide Billy's name, and when the judges show up all we have to do is grin and act proud. Nerds get all tongue-tied. The judges will read the posters, and boom, we get first prize!"

"Hello, gentlemen," an adult said from behind them.

Both Bulk and Skull spun around, trying not to look guilty. "Um, hi," Skull said.

There were two judges, a man and a woman. They wore name tags: MR. NORDLING and MS. HERNANDEZ. "Interesting-looking project you have there," Ms. Hernandez said. "Why don't you tell us a little about what it does?"

"Um," Bulk said.

"Yeah, um . . ." Skull couldn't figure out what to say. Why had Bulk had this dumb idea? "The poster says it better than I could," he said, pointing to one of the posters.

"Targeted anti-dimensional energy coherence disrupter," Mr. Nordling read. "That's a mouthful, ah, what are your names? I don't see them on your table anywhere."

"I'm Billy," Skull said.

Bulk glared at him. Skull couldn't figure out why he was mad at first, but then it hit him: They were supposed to be taking credit for the experiment, and he'd just messed it up by saying that his name was actually Billy!

Then he had another idea. If they couldn't take credit for Billy's experiment, the next best thing would be to mess it up for him so he couldn't win.

"Um," Skull said. The judges were watching, making him nervous.

"I'm Billy, too," Bulk said. "We're both, um, named Billy."

Ms. Hernandez was looking at her clipboard. It had a list of the experiments on it. "Billy . . . Cranston, is it?"

"That's me," both Bulk and Skull said at the same time.

Mr. Nordling and Ms. Hernandez looked at each other.

"Neither of you is Trini?" Ms. Hernandez asked.

Now it was Bulk and Skull's turn to look at each

other. "He is," Skull said, pointing at Bulk. Bulk glared at him, confused by the turn of events.

Mr. Nordling watched this exchange. He wrote something on his clipboard. "How about this," he said. "We're going to look at some other experiments and give you two a chance to get settled in."

"Sure," Skull said. "Okay. We'll get settled in."

"Yeah," Bulk said.

The judges moved on to another table, and Bulk punched Skull hard in the arm. "What are you doing, dummy? Now they think I'm Trini!"

"What was I supposed to do?" Skull asked. "We can't both be Billy."

"There goes my great idea," Bulk grumbled.

"Ha. Some great idea," Skull said. "How were you going to convince anyone you were Billy Cranston? Let's get back to our experiment before we get in trouble."

"What we should do is go find Billy and tell him the judges already came to his table," Bulk said.

Skull chuckled. "Oh yeah. That's a good idea. It'll be fun to watch him squirm."

They left the gym and looked down both of the hallways leading into other parts of the school.

"Wonder where he is," Bulk said.

"I bet he's in one of the science labs," Skull said. "Probably forgot some kind of nerd thing there and that's why he wasn't at his table."

"Right," Bulk said. "Let's check it out."

Chapter 10

From the throne room, Lord Zedd watched Goldar fighting the Red Ranger. "Why can you not destroy a single Power Ranger, you useless fool?" Zedd screamed.

He had sent Goldar when he saw Jason Scott isolated and alone. The Red Ranger was the leader of the team, and Lord Zedd was convinced the Power Rangers would fall apart if he could eliminate their leader. Surely Goldar should have been able to accomplish that!

But if not . . . if Goldar was just a bumbling idiot . . . then Lord Zedd was prepared to take matters into his own hands.

That was why he had chosen to create Wormazam. Lord Zedd had studied Earth's life-forms and learned that the earthworm had the power of regeneration. His Wormazams would take this to the next level. When his worm was cut in two, both halves would regrow into complete earthworms. It was a perfect way to keep the rest of the Power Rangers occupied while Lord Zedd focused on the Red Ranger. He knew they would fight Wormazam, and he also had guessed that they would resort to their weapons when they could not defeat Wormazam hand to hand.

His plan had worked perfectly. Now Wormazam had grown back to its full power, and there were four smaller Wormazams on the run in the school. The other Power Rangers would have their hands full chasing those Wormazams. They would not be able to come to the Red Ranger's aid.

Lord Zedd knew Baboo and Squatt were hiding behind the wall in the throne room. "You ran from the Power Rangers even though I surrounded you with the most powerful Z-Putties that have ever existed! I will destroy the Red Ranger myself, and the rest of the team will fall! Rita Repulsa would have failed already, but I have cut off the leader of the Power Rangers from all his friends! When he falls, the rest of the team will fall."

He pounded a fist into the wall and imagined Baboo and Squatt cowering. "The Power Rangers will be destroyed! And when I have destroyed them, I will hunt down their base. Zordon will be next, and that ridiculous robot Alpha 5. All will surrender, or I will annihilate them! Earth will be mine!"

Lord Zedd raised his staff. Then he paused. "Perhaps after this is all done . . . after I have seized this planet and made it mine . . . I will bring Rita out of the space Dumpster. Just long enough to see the look of miserable defeat on her face once more, and then I will put her back in the space Dumpster forever . . . with all her cowardly minions!" He pointed his staff at the throne-room window, where Earth shone blue and white. A crackle of energy surrounded him. When the flash faded, he was gone.

Chapter 11

Down in his laboratory, Finster heard Lord Zedd raging in the throne room. He had been working on his device for hours, and now he thought it was just about complete. And just in time. Lord Zedd was threatening to put them all in the space Dumpster with Rita Repulsa!

Finster vowed that he would not be going into the space Dumpster. Baboo and Squatt could take care of themselves. As far as Finster knew, they had not told Lord Zedd about the device, so Finster would be able to take complete credit for what was about to happen.

The device was designed to find the electronic frequency Alpha 5 used to send and receive messages. He used the same frequencies to talk to the Power Rangers and to Zordon. Finster had spent a long time finding that frequency. Then, once he had found it, he had to figure out a way to create a device that would use that same frequency. The third step was the most difficult and the most satisfying. Once Finster had found the frequency and built his device, he had to program it to send signals that Alpha 5 would be forced to obey—and cut off Alpha 5's ability to communicate with the Power Rangers.

Now he had done it! The device was complete. Already it was interfering with the Power Rangers' communications. He had built a glowing sphere that showed the waves of energy coming from the device. The wave patterns told Finster what the device was doing and what frequencies it controlled. All he had to do was focus it on the correct frequency, and Alpha 5 would be unable to resist.

Finster looked around. Baboo and Squatt were nowhere to be found. This irritated him. He wanted them to be present when he took control of Alpha 5. They should know that he was more useful and more powerful than they were.

He also wished Lord Zedd were there. Once Zedd saw what Finster had done, he would never banish Finster. Perhaps he would even let Finster stay at his side in the throne room, as Goldar always did. Finster was about to give him the key that would unlock the

Power Rangers' Command Center. Surely there would be a reward! Or at least the device would keep Finster out of the space Dumpster.

All he needed was a few minutes to make some final adjustments.

Chapter 12

Billy and Trini made the rounds of the auditorium, the pool, the choir room, the band room, and all the other spaces in that wing of the school. Everything seemed normal for a Saturday morning. Most of the rooms were empty, and a swim class for little kids in the pool was breaking up as Billy and Trini stuck their heads in. They did see Bulk and Skull wandering around near the band room, but there was no sign of any nefarious activity from Lord Zedd. So they decided to head back to the gym to see what was up with the rest of the team.

"Why haven't we heard from anybody?" Trini wondered. She raised her communicator but all she could hear was static. "Some kind of interference. That must be it. Look, we'll keep searching later. You've got to get back to your experiment."

Billy was anxious to return to the gym. The fair was starting, and he had to be there when the judges wanted to talk about his experiment. But his first responsibility was to the Power Rangers, and he had to live up to it. The conflict had him on edge. Trini could see it.

"Hey," she said. "It's going to be all right. We'll figure this out, and then we'll get you behind your . . . What is it again?" She had helped him put parts of his experiment together, but she still didn't completely understand what it was supposed to do. Billy's ideas were brilliant but pretty hard to follow sometimes.

"Targeted anti-dimensional energy coherence disrupter." Billy headed straight for his table when they came into the gym.

Trini quickly caught up to him and spent a minute reading the posters. "Right. Targeted anti-dimensional energy coherence disrupter. So let me guess, it jams signals, right?"

"It uses quantum energies from this dimension to detect and jam devices that use dimensional energy," Billy said. "Rita sometimes used those kinds of energy. I bet Lord Zedd does, too, but I haven't had a chance to really analyze the latest energy signals."

"So you're going to tell the judges you built it to fight a secret threat from space?" Trini wasn't sure how that would come across.

"I hadn't really thought about that yet." Billy looked around. "Where are the judges?"

"I'm more worried about where the rest of the team is," Trini said. "Is the disrupter already working? Maybe that's what's messing with our communicators. Come on. Let's make sure they're okay."

"Power Rangers," Zordon warned. Static crackled from her wrist-communicator. "Power Rangers," Zordon said again. They could barely make out what he was saying. "The Red Ranger is battling Goldar in the parking lot. You must go to his aid."

She and Billy looked around to see if anyone had noticed. But as the science fair got going, teams, judges, and spectators were all making so much noise that nobody had heard Zordon. Trini held her wrist up and spoke as quietly as she could. "Understood, Zordon. We're on our way. Did you hear that, Billy?"

He was already coming around the table. "Yeah. Goldar. Jason's going to need our help. Hey, where *are* Zack, Kimberly, and Tommy?"

Chapter 13

Zack, Kimberly, and Tommy had started off fighting one Wormazam. Now they had five to deal with. Four were little, about the size of golden retrievers, and they moved fast around the science lab, trying to get behind the three Power Rangers.

"Stay tight to one another," Tommy said. "Back to back to back."

"Think they can keep regenerating?" Zack wondered. "I mean, if we go after the little ones with our weapons, will they just make more?"

"I don't think we can take the chance. We have to find another way to defeat them."

Kimberly lunged out and kicked away a little Wormazam. Zack and Tommy were fending off blows from the big Wormazam. The floor was slick with worm slime, and they had trouble keeping their footing.

"It's a little cramped in here, don't you think?"

Wormazam said. "Maybe we should find some more room!"

Two of the little Wormazams headed for the door. Kimberly and Zack ran after them, but they were already out in the hallway.

"Go get them!" Tommy yelled. "And shut the door! I'll try to hold these guys here."

Zack slammed the door. How was Tommy going to hold out against the monsters by himself? He didn't even have his full Green Ranger powers.

"We can't leave him in there," he said.

"We have to," Kimberly shot back. She spoke into her wrist-communicator. "Zordon, we've found the monster Lord Zedd created. It split into a bunch of little monsters, and we're hunting them in the school."

"You . . . hurry," Zordon said through flares of static. "The Red Ranger . . . Goldar, but . . . divided, Lord Zedd . . . strike again."

Kimberly wasn't completely sure what he was saying, but it sounded like things were getting dangerous.

The little Wormazams were both headed back down the hall, toward the big lobby area between the classroom wing and the side of the building where the auditorium and the gym were.

"We can't let them get close to people," the Pink Ranger said. "They might cause a panic or wreck one of the experiments and start a fire."

"I know!" The Black Ranger ran after them . . . and right at that moment, Bulk and Skull came sprinting around the corner from the other side of the school at full speed.

"Whoa," Bulk said. "Power Rangers!"

Skull pointed at the two smaller Wormazams—who didn't look so little out in the hallway where you couldn't see the big one. "And monsters!"

They turned and ran back the way they had come. Kimberly took the chance to tackle one of the small Wormazams. Following her lead, Zack jumped on the other one. The Wormazams thrashed, but the Power Rangers held tight.

"Okay, now we've got them," Zack said. "What do we do with them?"

"Rangers," Zordon said through their wrist-communicators. "I have analyzed what Lord Zedd did. Wormazam's biology is based on a normal earthworm." Static flared again. ". . . dry out in the sun . . . destroy the original Wormazam, and the smaller ones will be destroyed, too."

"Then all we have to do is keep them out of the way while we go after the big one." Zack grunted. "I have an idea."

He ran up the hall and around the corner. Kimberly followed. The Wormazam in her arms slapped at her faceplate, leaving trails of slime. Zack reached the open janitorial closet. He threw in his Wormazam and kicked the mop bucket out of the way so he could slam the door.

"Your turn," he said to Kimberly. "Do it fast before the other one gets out."

"Got it," she said. Zack shoved open the door, and she flung in the Wormazam. It hit the back wall over the sink with a splat. Zack slammed the door again. They both heard the Wormazams mashing themselves against the door.

"Think they can turn the knob?" Zack wondered.

"I don't know. They don't seem too smart," Kimberly said. "Plus they're probably too slimy to make it turn."

"Still, we should make sure," Zack said. "I'll stay here and guard them. You go help Tommy. And we all need to think up some way to get rid of the big one."

"Okay," Kimberly said. She ran back toward the science lab. Over her shoulder she said, "Make sure you let us know if they get out again."

"I will," he said. "Go!"

Chapter 14

Zedd appeared in the canyon near the Red Ranger's Thunderzord and the fallen Goldar. "Goldar, get up!" he screamed.

The Thunderzord turned its head. "Yes, Red Ranger," Lord Zedd said, raising one clawed hand. "Lord Zedd is here to destroy you!"

He surrounded himself with a brilliant flare of light and grew until he was the same size as the Thunderzord.

"Your Thunderzord is no match for my powers!" Lord Zedd pointed his staff at the Thunderzord, and a blaze of energy burst out, blasting the Thunderzord and pushing it against the canyon wall. More rocks tumbled down from it.

Inside the Thunderzord, Jason was briefly stunned by the blast . . . and by the appearance of Lord Zedd. Unlike Rita Repulsa, Zedd never fought his own battles. This was something new, a challenge unlike any the Power Rangers had faced before. But that was all right. As long as they stuck together, they could handle anything.

He got the Thunderzord under control again, and turned it to face Lord Zedd. "You're seeing this, right, Zordon?"

Zordon's voice was grave. "Yes, Red Ranger. Zedd is a deadly opponent. Beware of his staff. It has a number of different powers."

The Thunderzord, still in Warrior Mode, picked up a boulder and threw it at Lord Zedd, who blasted it to gravel with his staff.

"The other Power Rangers are battling the monster Zedd created in the school," Zordon went on. "You must hold out against Zedd until help arrives."

"Goldar!" Lord Zedd screamed again. "Get on your feet!"

Goldar stirred and started to get to his feet. A falling rock bounced off his shoulder.

"Oh, Lord Zedd," he said. "Now that you are here, the Power Rangers won't stand a chance!"

Lord Zedd pointed his staff at the Red Ranger. "Don't just stand there. Attack!"

More boulders slid down from the canyon rim.

Goldar ducked, and they crashed around him, but Jason knew they wouldn't stop him for long. "Now I've got Goldar to deal with, too," Jason said. "Power Rangers! Where are you?"

Zack was first to answer. "I'm guarding two of the little Wormazams."

"Billy and I are on our way to help you," Trini called.

Tommy and Kimberly didn't answer.

"Wormazams?" Jason echoed.

"That's the monster Lord Zedd created," Zack said. "It calls itself Wormazam. And it split up into a bunch of little monsters. We just stuck some of them in a closet. I'll be there as soon as we make sure they can't get out."

"Stay and guard them if you have to," Jason said. "I can handle this."

Goldar crashed into him from the side, but Jason's Thunderzord shoved him away. "Afraid to face me on your own, Lord Zedd?" he challenged.

"You flatter yourself, Power Ranger," Lord Zedd said, laughing. "Lord Zedd fears nothing!"

He raised his staff again, in both hands this time. Energy began to crackle around its Z-shaped head. At that moment, Billy and Trini appeared in their Blue and Yellow Ranger suits. They both charged toward Lord Zedd. Trini landed a karate chop on his elbow, and the energy around the head of the staff fizzled out. Billy was right behind her, whirling through the air to land a kick on his other shoulder. The surprise attack caught Lord Zedd off guard, but he gathered himself and swatted them both to the ground with his staff.

"Goldar!" he barked. "Destroy these Rangers, and leave the Red Ranger to me. The rest will be easy once he is defeated."

So that's his plan, Jason thought. *That's why he finally decided to come down to Earth himself and take us on directly. He thinks that if he can bring down the Red Ranger, the rest of the Power Rangers will fall apart.*

That didn't worry Jason. He believed in himself, and he wasn't afraid to face Lord Zedd. But he also knew that the Power Rangers were a team. The Red Ranger might be the leader, but every member of the team was just as important. Lord Zedd, who ruled through fear, would never understand that.

Teamwork was the Power Rangers' biggest strength. That was what let them create the Power Blaster. That was what let them create the Thunder

Megazord. When the chips were down, the Power Rangers banded together.

Goldar leaped across the canyon floor and landed with an earthshaking boom near the Yellow and Blue Rangers, putting himself between them and Lord Zedd. He towered over them, brandishing his sword, but they faced him, unafraid. Jason heard the Yellow Ranger's voice.

"We'll lead Goldar away," she said. "Can you handle Lord Zedd?"

We'll find out, Jason thought. But he couldn't let the rest of the Power Rangers hear his uncertainty. "I've got this," he said. "You guys get up the canyon."

Together, the Blue and Yellow Rangers flashed into a quick teleport up to the head of the canyon. Goldar stomped after them, raising his sword to attack. Jason took his chance. The Red Dragon Thunderzord scooped up another huge boulder and threw it at Goldar. The boulder struck Goldar square in the back and knocked him flat on his face. Then the impact caused another landslide that buried him under tons of stone.

"Yeah, Red Ranger!" the Blue Ranger said. "We'll call our Thunderzords and join you!"

"We'll all need to face Lord Zedd together," Jason said. "But we can't have monsters loose in the school. That's your first objective."

"Prepare to face Lord Zedd, Red Ranger . . . and prepare to face your ultimate doom!" Lord Zedd's voice boomed through the canyon.

Jason knew he had to take a stand against Lord Zedd before Goldar dug himself out of the landslide. In Warrior Mode, the Tyrannosaurus Red Dragon Thunderzord spun to face him again. It raised its staff in a challenge. Lord Zedd raised his own staff in defiance, and the battle was on.

Chapter 15

Bulk and Skull knew the Power Rangers were in the school somewhere. That was a lot more interesting than the science fair. Skull had the idea that if they could get a picture of the monsters, they could probably sell it for a lot of money. Also, if they were lucky, they would find out who the Power Rangers really were.

"I think they went back this way," Skull said, pointing up the hallway away from the gym.

Ahead of them, they heard a bang like something had just hit one of the classroom doors from the inside.

"That's the spot," Bulk said.

They got to the door. It was a science lab. Bulk and Skull had both taken a class in there. They didn't remember much about it, though. School wasn't something they paid a lot of attention to.

"Let's check it out," Skull said. He opened the door.

One of the monsters came flying out and knocked

Bulk over. A split second later, another one followed it, knocking Bulk over again. Skull stood amazed . . . and then he was scared, as the monsters turned and slapped their tentacle-like arms against a bank of lockers. They were looking right at him.

They started to get closer. Bulk was trying to get to his feet, but he had so much slime all over him, he kept slipping. Skull grabbed his shirt and tried to pull him up. They both slipped again and hit the floor. "Oh man, this is it," Skull moaned. The two monsters were almost close enough to get them . . .

The Green Power Ranger came flying through the doorway and smashed into one of the monsters. It hit the lockers with a splat. The other lashed out its arms and grabbed his legs. He jackknifed and pounded away at it, kicking free. The first monster jumped on his back. He grabbed it with both hands and brought it down with another slimy splat on the floor.

Bulk and Skull had gotten to their feet. That was too much. They ran.

Chapter 16

The Black Ranger was fidgeting outside the janitorial closet, anxious to join the real fight. The little Wormazams couldn't get out of the closet; that was clear. If they could have, they would have already. Static flared out of his wrist-communicator, but he couldn't tell who was trying to get through. He raised his wrist, trying to hear. Then Bulk and Skull came skidding around the corner from the direction of the science classroom. They goggled at the Black Ranger.

"Another Power Ranger!" Bulk said.

A moment later, the Green Ranger, knotted in the arms of both little Wormazams from the science lab, came thrashing down the hall and barreled into the wall. Bulk and Skull started running again. The little Wormazams had the Green Ranger down. The Black Ranger ran to help. They let the Green Ranger go and attacked the Black Ranger instead, slapping at him with their powerful arms. Each blow was like getting pounded with a big rubber hose. By themselves they didn't hurt that much, but taken all together, they added up to quite a beating. The Black Ranger hung on and fought back against the Wormazams when he could.

The Green Ranger knocked one of the little Wormazams off the Black Ranger and kicked it away against the lockers on the other side of the hall.

The other one kept beating on the Black Ranger, but by itself it couldn't slow him down for long. He got back to his feet and started fighting back. It was like punching a rubber ball, but eventually the mini Wormazam started to wear down . . .

And then the pair of little Wormazams showed they had more surprises in store. They jumped at each other, tangled their limbs together—and merged into a single, larger Wormazam!

The Black Ranger thought of the janitorial closet. "Uh-oh," he said. "You think the ones in the closet did this, too?"

He and the Green Ranger tried to keep the Wormazam cornered, but now that it was bigger, they had to be more careful.

"I don't know," the Green Ranger said. "But if we put them all back together, they sure would be easier to keep track of."

"Also harder to fight, maybe?" The Black Ranger wasn't sure it was a good idea. "These things could do a lot of damage to regular people. We have to keep them away from the fair . . . starting with this one."

They grabbed it and started wrestling it down the hall toward the janitorial closet.

"When does the science fair start?" the Green Ranger asked.

The Black Ranger grunted with the effort of holding on to the Wormazam. "I think it already started."

They got the Wormazam to the janitorial closet. The Green Ranger shoved the door open and felt it thump against the other creatures inside. The Black Ranger pushed the Wormazam in, and the Green Ranger slammed the door.

"Let's find Jason," the Black Ranger said. "Hopefully this holds them for now."

"One thing we have to check first," the Green Ranger said. He ran back to the science classroom, the Black Ranger right with him. "That's what I was afraid of," the Green Ranger said. "I had to help Bulk and Skull, but when I came out . . ."

They both looked through the classroom door.

Wormazam had escaped.

Chapter 17

Finster was ready. He had made all the final adjustments, and the timing was perfect. Lord Zedd battled the Thunderzord down on Earth. In a moment he would see how useful Finster could be. Certainly Finster could do more to help Zedd than any worm creature. Finster was a genius, after all! Rita Repulsa had recognized his brilliance. He had to make Lord Zedd recognize it, too, or he was going to end up inside a space Dumpster next to Rita Repulsa sooner or later.

All he had to do now was aim the antenna. He worked a lever on his lab table, and outside the Moon Palace, an antenna shifted and pointed across space toward Angel Grove. When Finster had it locked in, he made one last check to see that he had all the settings correct.

He did, of course.

He pushed the button. The device came to life.

A beam of orange light shot out from the antenna across thousands of miles of space. It hit the Power Rangers' Command Center, high in the hills outside Angel Grove.

Finster watched the glowing sphere to see if the device was working. A moment later, he smiled and rubbed his hands together as the wave pattern showed he had found the right frequency.

"Yes," he said. "I have done it!"

He whirled around to see if Baboo and Squatt were there. They weren't, but he had a feeling they were watching from somewhere nearby.

"You see?" he called out. "I have done it!"

Then he returned to the machine. Alpha 5 was his to control . . . and it was time to start issuing commands.

Chapter 18

"Okay," the Pink Ranger said. She had joined up with Trini and Billy, and all three Rangers stood at the head of the canyon. "Maybe we should head back to the school and finish off Wormazam so we can focus on Lord Zedd."

"If we defeat the big Wormazam, all the little ones will disappear," the Blue Ranger said.

"Yeah, that's what Zordon said, right?" The Pink Ranger looked around.

"But if Goldar digs out from under that rockslide, we're going to need to call our Thunderzords," the Blue Ranger said.

"I think so, too," the Yellow Ranger said. "We need to take our chances. Let's take care of Wormazam before that happens."

There was a flash of light from up in the sky. For a moment the Power Rangers thought it was one of the monsters or one of Lord Zedd's minions. The flash of light had looked like his teleportation power.

But no other monster or enemy appeared. In fact, things got quieter. It took them a minute to figure out why. The Pink Ranger pointed. "What's wrong with Jason's Thunderzord?"

The Tyrannosaurus Red Dragon Thunderzord sat limp against the canyon wall below them.

"What happened?" the Black Ranger wondered.

"Rangers!" the Green Ranger called from inside the school. "Wormazam is loose in the school! And I can't get through to Zordon."

"Jason's Thunderzord is down," the Pink Ranger said. "It didn't get hit; it just . . . went limp."

"Alpha 5," the Blue Ranger said. "What's wrong with the Tyrannosaurus Red Dragon Thunderzord? Why can't we get through to Zordon?"

"Aye-yi-yi-yi-yi-yi . . . aye . . . yi-yi-yi-yi . . ." Static flared and cut off Alpha 5.

"I'm going to the Command Center," the Green Ranger said. "Sounds like something's wrong with Alpha 5. That's a lot of *yi*s. And since I can't summon a Thunderzord, anyway . . ."

The Green Ranger's powers had been low for some time. He could morph and use the Dragon

Dagger, but not his Thunderzord. Zordon and Alpha 5 were still trying to discover why. So if he couldn't help the rest of them regain access to their Thunderzords out here, it made sense for him to see what he could do in the Command Center.

"What about Wormazam?" the Pink Ranger asked.

"I'll handle Wormazam," the Black Ranger said.

Below them, Lord Zedd advanced on the fallen Thunderzord. "That's it," the Yellow Ranger said. "Sabertooth Tiger Griffin Thunderzord Power!"

Nothing happened.

"Aye-yi-yi-yi-yi-yi . . ." Alpha 5's voice was barely audible through the static from the Command Center. To the Blue Ranger, it sounded like Alpha 5 was stuck in some kind of loop . . . and all of a sudden the interference was only focused on the Command Center . . .

"I have to get to the gym!" the Blue Ranger shouted. The rest of the team looked at him. How could that be more important than the threat of Lord Zedd?

"The flash of light. It was a signal. Alpha 5 has been hacked! That's why he's stuck in a loop, saying 'aye-yi-yi' over and over again. That's why we can't call our Thunderzords and why Jason's won't work.

My experiment can counter the attack," the Blue Ranger went on. "That's what I built it for! I just didn't know I would need it so soon."

"Are you sure?" the Yellow Ranger asked. She was ready to take the fight to Lord Zedd right there, Thunderzords or no Thunderzords. The odds would be against them, but they had to do something.

"One hundred percent," the Blue Ranger said. "I know I can do this. I just need a minute to readjust the disrupter."

"What is the experiment, anyway?" the Pink Ranger asked.

"It's a targeted anti-dimensional energy coherence disrupter," Billy said.

The Pink Ranger paused. "A what?"

"It finds enemy signals and jams them," the Yellow Ranger explained. "Like radio jamming, only it targets dimensional energy signals instead of radio waves."

Below them, the Red Ranger appeared next to his fallen Thunderzord. Lord Zedd advanced toward him. "I hear you, team," the Red Ranger said. "Billy, if you think you can get Alpha 5 back online, do it."

The Blue Ranger disappeared, teleporting to the back wall of the school, where he could morph back to his normal appearance without anyone seeing him.

"You and me," the Yellow Ranger said to the Pink Ranger. "Let's go."

They took off down the canyon, jumping from rock to rock, down to where Jason was facing Lord Zedd. But they only got halfway there before Goldar reared up out of the rockslide, directly in their path.

Chapter 19

With his Thunderzord out of commission, Jason did the only thing he could do: He teleported away from the Thunderzord and appeared directly in front of Lord Zedd.

"I don't know what you did to knock out my Zord," he said, "but you know what? It's not going to matter. The Power Rangers are going to take you down with or without Zords."

Zedd threw back his head and laughed as he shrank back to his normal size. The sound reminded Jason of a rockslide.

"What Power Rangers? I only see the Red Ranger. Do you see your team around you?"

Jason knew he was alone, and he also knew the rest of the team was fighting as hard as they could against other threats. Zedd had maneuvered them all so he could take on Jason alone.

"My team is doing what they're supposed to do:

Defend Earth," he said. "And that's what I'm going to do."

"No, Red Ranger. You are going to bow to Lord Zedd . . . or you are going to be destroyed. Those are your choices. Choose now."

"Bowing isn't really my style," Jason said.

Up the canyon a few hundred yards, the Yellow and Pink Rangers were mixing it up with Goldar. The Blue Ranger was at the science fair. The Black Ranger was chasing Wormazam, and the Green Ranger was . . . well, with any luck he was figuring out what went wrong back at the Command Center.

That left the Red Ranger, standing toe-to-toe with Lord Zedd.

"If you will not bow, I will end this battle with my foot on your neck," Lord Zedd sneered. He raised his staff, and the ground heaved under the Red Ranger's feet. He backflipped away from the shock wave and landed a little farther from Lord Zedd.

"You can't get away from me, Red Ranger!" Zedd cackled.

"What makes you think I'm trying to get away from you?" Jason shot back. "I just needed a running start."

He sprinted forward and launched himself into a

twisting somersault. As he came down toward Lord Zedd, he gripped Zedd's staff with two hands and used it as leverage to smash a spinning kick into the side of Lord Zedd's helmet.

Lord Zedd thrashed away from him, and Jason lost his grip on the staff. He hit the ground hard, but he had gotten in a good shot. He rolled to one side as Zedd brought the head of the staff down like a poleax. The Z crackled and spat energy as it sliced a rock in two, right where Jason's head had been a split second before.

It was time to up the ante a little. Jason held up his right hand.

"Power Sword!" he called out. His Power Sword shimmered to life, appearing in his hand. He spun it around once, feeling its weight and balance.

Lord Zedd nodded. "Your last resort," he growled. "Good! Tap all your powers! That way when you are defeated, you will know you never had a chance."

He swung his staff, and Jason parried it. The impact jarred his arms all the way to the shoulders. Lord Zedd was a cruel blowhard, but he was also very powerful. Jason fought back with everything he had. The Power Rangers were depending on him.

Earth itself was depending on him.

Spinning away from Lord Zedd's next attack, he struck back. His blade glanced off Zedd's armor in a shower of sparks. With his staff in both hands, Zedd knocked Jason sprawling. Again Jason got up before Lord Zedd could finish him off. He was below Zedd on the slope of the canyon wall now. Zedd advanced, pushing him farther down toward the canyon floor. Jason parried and countered. When they got to the canyon floor, the ground would be level again. Then he would make his next move.

Unless Billy could break the hold over Alpha 5. Then they would be able to call their Thunderzords.

Until then, he had to hold on.

Chapter 20

The Black Ranger was left to hunt Wormazam after the Green Ranger had teleported away. With all the mini Wormazams pinned inside the janitorial closet, he followed the trail of slime toward the gym. He had to catch Wormazam before the monster could cause havoc at the crowded science fair.

Following the slime, he spotted Wormazam approaching an intersection in the hallway. To the right, it headed toward the pool and to the left left, toward the gym. The Black Ranger ran forward and drove his shoulder into Wormazam from behind, pushing the monster through the intersection and down the dim stretch of hallway in the direction of the pool. There was nobody there. Wormazam immediately wrapped the Black Ranger up in its tail, smashing him against a row of lockers. Some burst open, spilling books and coats out onto the floor. The Black Ranger fought back, trying to get a grip on its arms. He was so covered in slime that it was hard to keep on his feet.

Just when he'd gotten a grip on it, Wormazam disappeared in a flash of light.

The Black Ranger stood in the quiet hallway. From one direction, he heard the sounds of the science fair echoing from the gym.

From the other direction, he heard a constant banging. Like something was stuck inside a room and trying to get out. He spoke into his wrist-communicator. "Wormazam disappeared," he said. "Should I head your way?"

"Make sure the other ones can't get out first," the Red Ranger responded. "If they get out . . ."

"Okay," the Black Ranger said. He ran back toward the janitorial closet, wondering what he would find.

Next to the janitorial closet was an English classroom, its walls lined with steel bookcases. The shelves were jammed with heavy hardcover books. The Black Ranger dragged one of the bookcases out of the room and shoved it up against the closet door. The Wormazams thrashed and banged inside. He went and got another one, then added a table that he tipped on its side. In a minute he had a huge pile of furniture jammed up against the door.

"Hey," he said. "Wormazams: Come on out."

Was it one Wormazam or several? Maybe they had all merged back together. He didn't know. Either way, the banging from inside the closet wasn't moving the furniture.

"Okay, team," he called out. "I'm coming your way." In a ripple of teleportation energy, he was gone.

Chapter 21

When the Green Ranger appeared in the Command Center, he morphed back to his regular appearance. He was still worried about his energy levels and wanted to make sure he would have enough power to use the Dagger if the need arose. The first thing he saw was Alpha 5, standing in front of the long bank of computer terminals.

"Aye-yi-yi-yi-yi," he said.

Whoa, Tommy thought. *Four* yis. That meant Alpha 5 was distressed. "Alpha," he said. "What are you doing? Jason's Thunderzord is deactivated!"

"Aye-yi-yi-yi-yi," Alpha 5 said again.

"He knows we are under attack," Zordon boomed. Tommy turned to look at the giant screen where Zordon's face always appeared. The ancient mentor of the Power Rangers looked worried. "But he is under someone else's command. Communications from the Command Center are severed. I do not think

Lord Zedd could have done this. I suspect it is Finster. No one else among Zedd's minions has his inventive capability."

"Can we shut him down?" Tommy asked. "He's not attacking me. Maybe he would let me deactivate him or something."

"That would not undo what he has done," Zordon said.

"Then what can we do?" Tommy asked. "Billy is trying something with the science experiment he already built, but what if that doesn't work?"

"The only other thing to do is go to the Moon Palace and try to find out what Finster has done," Zordon answered. "But your powers, reduced as they are, will not be strong enough to teleport you there."

"I'm willing to try," Tommy said. He would do anything to help out the team, and they needed Zordon. How could they fight Lord Zedd without him? And without their Thunderzords?

"If I could route some energy from the Morphin Grid to you . . . no, it isn't possible. Alpha 5 must execute those commands, and he is under Finster's control."

"There must be something I can do," Tommy said.

"Aye-yi-yi-yi-yi-yi!" Alpha 5 cried out. Tommy counted five *yi*s that time. What did that mean? Did Alpha 5 know what was happening even though he couldn't do anything about it?

He ran to Alpha 5 and grabbed the robot by his shoulders.

There was a flash, and the next thing Tommy knew, he was lying on his back on the floor. Alpha 5 had shocked him. Tommy wasn't sure if he was attacking, but he wasn't going to let anyone get close, either.

But he didn't sound happy about it. "Aye-yi-yi-yi-yi!" Alpha 5 spun in a circle. A little curl of smoke rose from the spot on his chassis where Tommy had touched him.

Tommy got to his feet. "Wait," Zordon said. "Give the Blue Ranger a chance. You are fighting bravely. Trust one another, and believe you can defeat Lord Zedd . . . even without my help."

Chapter 22

Wormazam appeared on the canyon wall near Lord Zedd.

"I am Wormazam, here to destroy the Power Rangers!" it burbled, waving its arms. "Lord Zedd, which one should I destroy first?"

"Slimy worthless creature, how could you have failed to destroy them in the school? Not even one! Burrow into the ground and disappear!" Lord Zedd's temper got hotter and hotter the more his minions disappointed him. He had no wish to be distracted now, when he had the Red Ranger at his mercy.

"I am here, Lord Zedd! I am at your service!" Wormazam bowed.

"Then serve me by destroying the Power Rangers!" Zedd roared. He pointed up the canyon, where the Yellow and Pink Rangers were dodging Goldar's attacks. "Now! Leave the Red Ranger to me!"

"Yes, Lord Zedd!" Wormazam started squelching

its way toward them. For a creature made from a worm, it moved incredibly fast. It closed the distance to the two Power Rangers in a matter of seconds, and the battle was on.

The Black Ranger appeared at the head of the canyon a moment later. The Red Ranger saw him and called out, "Stay with the team! I'll handle Zedd!" The Black Ranger ran to help his fellow Rangers as Wormazam closed in. Goldar brought his sword down, crashing it into the rocks near the Yellow and Pink Rangers. They lost their footing and tumbled down among the rocks. The Pink Ranger kept going, somersaulting between Goldar's immense legs and coming up behind him.

"Power Bow!" she said. Her Power Bow appeared in her hands, and she fired two arrows at Goldar.

They exploded on Goldar's armor, and he turned to her, teeth bared. Behind him, Wormazam slid down the wall toward the Yellow Ranger, who was still getting to her feet. The Black Ranger intercepted it, and they grappled. Fighting Wormazam, it was difficult to use martial arts. Its arms whipped quickly around any block. The Black Ranger held his own and gave the Yellow Ranger time to rejoin the fight. Goldar was now focused on the Pink Ranger. He spread his wings and leaped toward her. She fired another arrow, staggering him.

Billy, she thought, *I sure hope you get that experiment up and running soon.*

Chapter 23

Billy morphed back to his everyday look when he appeared next to the back door of Angel Grove High School. He ran into the gym and wove through the crowds to his table.

The judges were two tables over, talking to each other in front of a display about Venus flytraps. Billy started tapping away at the keyboard attached to the disrupter. He only had it set up for a demonstration, and he was going to have to do some fast programming if he wanted it to break up the signal that was attacking Alpha 5.

He got lost in the program he was writing and only looked up when someone said, "Billy Cranston?"

The two judges were in front of his table: Mr. Nordlinger and Ms. Hernandez. "Um, yeah," Billy said. "That's me."

"We were about to move on without you, Billy," Mr. Nordlinger said. "You know you were supposed to stay at your table once the fair began, right?"

"I'm sorry," Billy said. He kept tapping out lines of code. He was almost done.

The two judges consulted their clipboards. "So," Ms. Hernandez said. "What exactly does this machine do, young man?"

"It's, um . . ." Billy hesitated. He wasn't sure how else to explain it. "Well," he said, "what the experiment does is it's a band-shifting frequency jammer designed to stop hackers from getting into your Wi-Fi," he said. "It detects signals that shouldn't be there and breaks them up." Inside he was cringing because he felt like he wasn't doing the experiment justice. But that was the best he could do at the moment.

"Interesting," Ms. Hernandez said. "And you made this yourself?"

"I did the programming stuff," Billy said. "My friend Trini did some soldering and put together the case. Oh, and she wrote the posters."

"Is she here?"

Billy looked around. "I don't see her. Does she have to be here?"

"Well, technically everyone involved in an experiment is supposed to be present at the judging conversation," Mr. Nordlinger said.

"Oh," Billy said. "Maybe she's in the bathroom. Do you want to come back?"

"I think we can proceed for now," Ms. Hernandez said. "Go ahead and show us how it works."

"Oh yeah," Billy said. "Thought you'd never ask."

He hit ENTER on the program and then he had to figure out what to tell the judges. But he also had to watch the monitors to make sure the disrupter had found the signal from Lord Zedd and broken it up.

As he stared at the monitors, one of the screens lit up. The disrupter had located the enemy signal! "There," he said, pointing.

"There what?" Mr. Nordlinger asked.

"Wait a second," Billy said. "I'm . . ." He clapped his hands. "Yes!"

Ms. Hernandez was watching the monitors. There were two, both divided into two displays. Each of the four screens showed something different. "Did it work?" she asked.

"It sure did," Billy said. He pointed at one of the screens. It displayed an image of smooth, intersecting curves. To calibrate the machine, last night he had captured a baseline of what the Command Center frequency band looked like when everything was running right.

"See? This is what the target signal band looked like before the, um . . ."

"Hackers," Ms. Hernandez said.

"Right, before the hackers tried to get in." Billy pointed at a second screen. The smooth curves were a different shape and a different color. "The color change is because the origin of the command signal is different. That's what the hackers were doing. They tried to pretend they were the regular command signal, and they fooled the security."

"You mean they were trying to get into the school's network?" Ms. Hernandez looked alarmed.

Billy looked over at her. He wanted to correct her and tell what had really happened, but he couldn't. Inside, he was lit up with the success. He'd done it! But he had to explain it to the judges in a way they would understand without actually telling a lie.

"It happens all the time," he said. "People are always trying to get ads and stuff onto pages even when you don't want them."

Mr. Nordlinger nodded. Neither of the judges were looking at him, though. They were studying the monitors. Billy reminded himself he was trying to win a science fair here, along with trying to save Alpha 5 and make sure the Power Rangers could use their Thunderzords to fight off Lord Zedd, Goldar, and Wormazam. It was a lot to keep in his head all at the same time.

"And here's what happens when the disrupter locates the hacker signal," he said.

A third screen showed the wave broken up into a crazy bunch of squiggles. The judges both nodded and made notes on their clipboards.

"The disrupter broke up the hacker signal so the target network could tell it was being attacked. And what happens here is that you can see the target network is restored to normal." Billy pointed at the fourth screen, which was keyed to the Command Center's frequency.

"That's the school network there?" Mr. Nordlinger aimed his pen at the same screen.

"The target network," Billy said, careful not to tell a lie to the judges.

He was dying to talk to the other Power Rangers and find out if Alpha 5 was working again, but he couldn't. Not until the judges left.

"And just so we have this straight," Ms. Hernandez said, "you designed and programmed this device yourself, correct?"

"Yes. Correct. But like I said before, Trini did some soldering and some of the work on the case design and stuff."

"Well," Mr. Nordlinger said. "This is quite impressive. You have a good future ahead of you in computer programming."

"Thank you," Billy said.

"Is there anything else you want to tell us about your experiment?" Ms. Hernandez asked. Both waited with pens poised over their clipboards.

Billy thought about that. What he wanted to tell them was that he had just defended Zordon's Command Center against an attack from hostile aliens. But he couldn't really do that, could he? He also wanted to say that he had to go and help his friends fight off a monster created from an earthworm in the Angel Grove High School science lab . . . but that wouldn't really go over very well, either.

So all he said was, "No, I think that's it. Um, thank you."

"Very nice, Billy," Ms. Hernandez said. "The

judges will have their final decision in an hour or so."

They moved on to another table. Billy watched them go, smiling at them in case they turned around again. Then, as soon as they had started talking to another student team, he ran for the door.

Chapter 24

In the Command Center, Alpha 5 stopped spinning. "Aye . . . yi?" he said. "Zordon, what happened to me?"

"Alpha 5! You're back?" Tommy took a step toward him but didn't touch him. He didn't want to risk getting zapped again.

"You were hacked, Alpha 5," Zordon said in a grave voice.

"Hacked? Aye-yi-yi, how did that happen?"

"We believe it was Finster. The Blue Ranger interrupted his energy signal and restored your control."

"Finster? Of course!" Alpha 5 said. "He's full of tricks."

"Quickly now, Alpha 5." Zordon was all business. "While Finster had control over you, the Thunderzords were deactivated. You must reactivate them immediately. Lord Zedd is in Angel Grove, and so are Goldar and the new creation, Wormazam."

"Yes, Zordon! Right away." Alpha 5 turned to the terminals and started working. "It will only take a moment."

Tommy watched, frustrated that he couldn't help. Would Alpha 5 get it done fast enough?

"Green Ranger," Zordon said. Tommy looked up at him. "You must go and help your fellow Power Rangers. Even if you cannot pilot a Thunderzord right now, you are still a member of this team, and they need you."

Zordon was right. Tommy nodded. "I'm on it, Zordon. You sure everything is all set here?"

"You are needed in the field, Green Ranger. I'll handlc things here."

"Then I'm gone," Tommy said. A moment later Alpha 5 had teleported him back to the canyon.

Chapter 25

The Red Ranger dodged another energy blast from Lord Zedd's staff. He was keeping Zedd's attention, which was good. So far he had also been able to either block Zedd's attacks or deflect the energy blasts with his Power Sword. But sooner or later, Zedd wasn't going to miss. The Rangers needed to break Finster's hold over Alpha 5 and get to their Thunderzords, or they were going to be in serious trouble.

"When I defeat you, Red Ranger, your team will crumble," Lord Zedd gloated. "I will stand triumphant over the Power Rangers—and then I will find your Command Center and destroy Zordon at last!"

"You're getting a little ahead of yourself, Zedd," the Red Ranger shot back. "First you have to defeat me, and I don't see you doing that."

He sounded more confident than he felt. Lord Zedd was pressing him to the limits of his fighting ability. Jason had the discipline to be at his best every time he had to fight. And he needed every bit of his skill and courage now. Zedd was out for blood.

Another blast from Lord Zedd's staff blew a large boulder into gravel as Jason dove out of the way and rolled. He came up with the sword in a defensive hold, and Zedd's staff clanged off the blade. Jason struck back, denting the armor on Lord Zedd's leg. Zedd roared, more in anger than pain, and brought the staff down again. It rang against the Power Sword and came grinding down the blade to lock against the hilt. Zedd leaned into Jason with all his strength, but Jason held his ground. He had the power of the Morphin Grid with him, and he would not yield.

Lord Zedd chuckled, and his staff changed into a giant snake. It struck out, coiling itself around the Red Ranger's arms and causing him to drop his sword. Its fangs scraped against his helmet.

So this is what Zordon meant when he warned me about the staff, Jason thought.

He got one arm free and grabbed the snake around the neck, holding it at arm's length. Slowly, using all his strength, he forced the snake to loosen its grip enough that he could get his other arm free.

Then he got his free hand on his sword.

"You're about to lose your snake, Zedd," he said through gritted teeth.

The snake disappeared, becoming a staff once again. The Red Ranger pivoted away from Lord Zedd, who overbalanced and fell forward. But he was quick on his feet, and before Jason could take advantage, Zedd was upright and facing him again.

"How long can you hold on, Red Ranger?" Zedd taunted him. "I grow stronger! If you have not defeated me yet, what hope do you have?"

Hope, Jason thought. "I don't need hope," he said. "I know I'm better than you. You keep coming at me, and sooner or later I'm going to win." He leveled the Power Sword at Lord Zedd. "Come on. Try me."

Zedd roared in fury and charged. He drove the Red Ranger back again with a series of strikes from his staff. Jason skipped back and dodged to the side, hoping Zedd would eventually wear himself out so Jason could counterattack.

But time was running out. Goldar and Wormazam were keeping the team separated, which was what Lord Zedd wanted. They needed to find a way to strike back and fight together, and Jason had to lead the way. He was the Red Ranger, and his friends were depending on him.

All the other Power Rangers, except Tommy, were now battling Goldar and Wormazam. Kimberly was still firing her bow up at Goldar, but Wormazam was getting close to her. Soon she would have to drop the bow and take him on hand to hand . . . or hand to slimy arm? Either way, they couldn't use weapons against Wormazam unless they wanted more little Wormazams running through the hills outside Angel Grove.

Jason saw the Blue Ranger in the group and called out, "Billy! Did it work?"

"I think so!"

The Green Ranger appeared between Jason and the rest of the group, up the canyon. "Tommy!" the Yellow Ranger called out. "We could use a hand here!"

Tommy ran to join the battle against Wormazam and Goldar. Wormazam scuttled up the slope and batted rocks down toward the Power Rangers fighting Goldar. Occasionally one of them hit Goldar, who roared at Wormazam. "Careful, worm!"

"That's Wormazam! And I throw rocks where I want! Get out of the way if you don't want to get hit!"

To emphasize his point, Wormazam leaned against a large boulder and sent it bouncing down to the canyon floor. It deflected off a tree and smashed into other rocks, nearly flattening the Black Ranger.

Goldar turned and saw the Green Ranger approaching. He hated Tommy more than the rest of the Power Rangers, and once he saw him, he forgot all about the others. He charged at Tommy, sword high and teeth bared. Each footstep shook the canyon floor.

"Bring it, gorilla boy!" the Green Ranger sang out. He ducked inside Goldar's wild sword swing and jumped up to grab on to Goldar's armored hand. He landed three quick punches to Goldar's thumb, loosening his grip on his sword. The sword spun away and stuck point-first in the canyon floor. Goldar tried to crush the Green Ranger with his other hand, but Tommy saw it coming and leaped away.

The Red Ranger hesitated briefly when he saw Goldar go after the Green Ranger, and the momentary distraction almost cost Jason dearly. He sensed something moving out of the corner of his eye and flung himself backward at the last moment before Lord Zedd's staff split the air an inch in front of his nose. The Red Ranger turned the backward flip into a handspring, landing on his feet again and launching a flurry of attacks that drove Lord Zedd back.

"Power Rangers," Zordon said. "We have restored control of the Command Center. Now is the time to summon your Thunderzords."

"Woo-hoo!" the Black Ranger yelled. "Here's where we turn the tide, Power Rangers!"

"Did you hear that, Zedd?" the Red Ranger shouted. "Your scheme didn't work. We've got our Thunderzords back, and you'd better be ready."

He teleported back to the Red Dragon Thunderzord. Lord Zedd prepared to grow again, anticipating the Thunderzords' attack . . . and Finster chose exactly that moment to appear.

"Lord Zedd! I wished to give you time to savor your victory over the Power Rangers before I appeared to accept your praise. By now I'm sure you have noticed the marvelous results of my machine. As you will have seen, it completely deactivates the Thunderzords . . ."

He looked up as he spoke. The Red Dragon Thunderzord was moving again.

"Finster," Lord Zedd growled. "Did you attack the Power Rangers' Command Center?"

"Yes, Lord Zedd. You see, I was able to commandeer Alpha 5 for him to . . . deactivate the Thunderzords . . ." Now Finster was looking confused.

"Silence!"

Finster fell silent.

"What you have done is waste a chance to take advantage of your machine. If you had told me about it, I could have made use of it. But now . . . now . . ." Lord Zedd loomed over Finster, who cowered and dropped to his knees. "Now the chance is wasted! You have ruined everything! This is all your fault!"

"I'm sorry, Lord Zedd. You see, I wanted to prove myself to you because of what, er . . . happened with Rita, and—"

"Silence!"

Lord Zedd held up a hand. "Listen, Finster."

Finster listened.

The Power Rangers were summoning their Thunderzords.

The Black Ranger called out, "Mastodon Lion Thunderzord Power!"

Then the Pink Ranger: "Pterodactyl Firebird

Thunderzord Power!"

And the Blue Ranger: "Triceratops Unicorn Thunderzord Power!"

The Yellow Ranger followed up: "Sabertooth Tiger Griffin Thunderzord Power!"

And then the Tyrannosaurus Red Dragon Thunderzord also stood up again. The Power Rangers were at full strength once more.

"Did you hear those sounds, Finster?" Lord Zedd asked. His voice was deadly quiet.

Finster nodded. "Yes, Lord Zedd. I heard them."

"Those," growled Lord Zedd, "were the sounds of a space Dumpster coming to get you! Now get out of my sight before you see me truly become angry! If I find you in the Moon Palace, I will . . ." Lord Zedd couldn't find a word horrible enough. He raised his staff, and energy began to flare around the Z at its head.

Finster vanished.

Lord Zedd turned to see the Red Dragon Thunderzord still stamping toward him. "Red Ranger!" he shouted. "You show your weakness! But I have driven you from your Thunderzord once and will do it again! Then, you will—"

He was interrupted when the Red Dragon Thunderzord took its dragon form again, sweeping into the sky and blasting Lord Zedd with its fiery breath. When the fire cleared, five Thunderzords lined the rim of the canyon, looking down on Goldar, Wormazam, and the raging Lord Zedd.

"Destroy them!" he screamed. Around him the earth was blackened and smoking. "Destroy them all!"

Chapter 26

As one, the Thunderzords advanced down the canyon toward Goldar, Wormazam, and Lord Zedd. Lord Zedd threw a grenade across the canyon to explode in a brilliant flash at Wormazam's feet.

"We need a much bigger creature!" Lord Zedd proclaimed. "The biggest!"

When the light had faded, Wormazam had grown to incredible size. He was bigger than any of the Thunderzords and the same size as Goldar, whose wings almost spanned the canyon from wall to wall when he spread them out. The two beckoned the Thunderzords closer. They were ready for the fight. They would have hated to miss it. Goldar clashed his sword against his armor, challenging the Power Rangers. The sound would have echoed off the walls of Angel Grove High School if he hadn't been deep in the canyon.

Wormazam wasn't as loud, but it was just as big.

The three ground-based Thunderzords rolled down into the canyon. "Get the legs!" the Black Ranger yelled into his helmet-communicator.

They could also hear Alpha 5. "Aye-yi-yi, look at the size of that worm thing!"

"I'm a little more worried about Goldar," Zack said.

Goldar's sword clanged off the armor of the Yellow Ranger's Sabertooth Tiger Griffin Thunderzord. The sound left Trini's ears ringing. "Me too!" she shouted. She blasted Goldar with fireballs.

From the rim of the canyon, the Green Ranger watched and seethed. He couldn't do anything when the other Power Rangers were in their Thunderzords! Then he looked over his toes, down into the canyon. The Tyrannosaurus Red Dragon Thunderzord swept in a long circle around Lord Zedd, who blasted away at it with the deadly energies of his staff.

Maybe I can help, Tommy thought. *Jason's been holding out against Lord Zedd all by himself for a long time now. And Zedd isn't three hundred feet tall.*

Lord Zedd was growing more and more frustrated with the Power Rangers. They should have been defeated by now! But the Red Ranger was stronger than Lord Zedd had given him credit for. And the other Power Rangers were holding their own against Goldar and Wormazam.

It was time for a change in tactics. "Wormazam, bring down the Red Thunderzord!" Lord Zedd raged.

"As you command, Lord Zedd!" Wormazam stepped back from the Sabertooth Tiger Griffin Thunderzord and turned toward the bottom of the canyon. The Red Dragon Thunderzord was turning to make another pass. Its mouth opened, and fire started to glow within.

Wormazam raised its arms and pointed them at the Red Dragon Thunderzord. A long double stream of wormy slime shot out from the ends of its arms.

"Man, I didn't know it could do that," the Blue Ranger said from inside the Triceratops Unicorn Thunderzord.

"Me neither," Trini said.

"It sure didn't do that inside," Zack said. "At least not that I saw."

The slime splattered across the Red Dragon Thunderzord's head.

"I can't see!" Jason cried out. The Red Dragon

Thunderzord crashed into the canyon wall and landed at the bottom with a huge rockslide cascading down around it. Inside, Jason bounced and crashed around. It was a bruising crash, and the Thunderzord would need some repairs.

"Okay, then," he said. "Let's settle this, Lord Zedd. Just you and me."

He tapped his coin and teleported out of the Thunderzord, appearing in front of Lord Zedd and surprising him. Jason didn't even use his sword this time. He put all his focus and all his discipline to work, concentrating on one thing and one thing only: defeating Lord Zedd.

Jason felt strong. He was inspired by seeing how the other Power Rangers had figured out how to meet the many challenges they had already faced that morning. They had stayed together, and each member of the team had done what was needed. Plus Billy had gotten to put on his show for the judges at the science fair.

Lord Zedd slashed at Jason with the staff, but Jason felt a little extra energy, as if the team was making him stronger. He evaded Lord Zedd's dangerous strikes with ease. The angrier Lord Zedd got, the more reckless he got. He charged after the Red Ranger, blasting at him and driving him closer to the opposite wall of the canyon.

"You have courage, Power Ranger," Lord Zedd said. "But courage does not matter if you do not have enough strength to back it up."

"Jason's got more strength than you'll ever know," said someone else, from just behind Lord Zedd. It was Tommy Oliver.

"You, Green Ranger?" Zedd sounded amused. "Are you not the Red Ranger's rival?"

The Green Ranger knew Lord Zedd was trying to drive a wedge between the Power Rangers by causing rivalries. That might have worked up in the Moon Palace, where Zedd ruled through fear . . . but it wasn't going to work down here. "We're a team," the Green Ranger answered. "That's all you need to know."

Chapter 27

Higher in the canyon, the four Thunderzords were slowly gaining the advantage against Goldar and Wormazam. The Firebird Thunderzord beat its wings, unleashing a vortex of wind that spun Goldar to the ground and knocked Wormazam into the canyon wall. The Unicorn and Griffin Thunderzords bombarded Goldar with fireballs and boulders. He flailed back at them, but his sword only whooshed through empty air. Wormazam writhed against the rocks, trying to get to its feet. The powerful wind began to dry out Wormazam. Its arms couldn't stretch far enough to strike at the Firebird Thunderzord. Its motions got slower and stiffer, and finally it froze in place, caked in dust. There was a burst of energy as Lord Zedd's power left it, and then Wormazam was gone.

"See, Lord Zedd?" the Red Ranger said. "We work well together."

Lord Zedd saw this. He looked back at the Red Ranger.

"You imagine you have won today, Red Ranger? A fatal mistake. You see a tiny part of a much greater plan, which will end in your ultimate defeat! But I will unfold it in my own time. You will see . . . and very soon."

Then Lord Zedd disappeared in a flash of light.

A moment later, Goldar disappeared, too.

The Blue Ranger appeared where Wormazam had been, looking down at something on the ground. It was a solitary earthworm, nosing its way along the bare earth. Kimberly, Zack, and Trini joined him a moment later. Billy watched the worm for a while, then dug a small hole in softer soil under a eucalyptus tree and dropped in the worm. "I mean, it's just a worm," he said as Jason and Tommy approached.

"Firebird Thunderzord did a number on Wormazam," Zack said.

"Early bird gets the worm," Kimberly cracked. They laughed.

Chapter 28

But Kimberly's joke reminded Zack and Trini of something. "The little Wormazams," they said simultaneously.

"Oh man," Tommy said.

Tapping their coins, Zack, Trini, and Tommy morphed and teleported to the school, appearing in the hall near the janitorial closet. It was quiet, and when they pushed the bookcases aside, they understood why.

The little Wormazams were gone, just as Zordon had anticipated . . . but they had left a lot of slime behind. "Ew," the Yellow Ranger said, looking at the line of goop.

As they stood in front of the door, Bulk and Skull appeared around the corner.

"Whoa!" Bulk said. "Power Rangers!"

"Man, it reeks in there," Skull said. "Or is that me?"

"Hey, you guys weren't around, so we took care of

the monsters ourselves," Bulk said. He dropped into a clumsy version of a Power Rangers fighting stance. "Good thing we were around, huh?"

Typical Bulk and Skull, thought the Green Ranger. *Taking credit for everything*. He didn't mind . . . but it did give him a thought. He took the mop out of the bucket just inside the door and thrust the handle into Skull's hand. "Sure is," he said. "But now you get to clean it up." Then he and the Yellow Ranger headed off down the hall, with the Black Ranger right behind them.

"Did you see that?" Skull turned to Bulk. "A Power Ranger gave me this mop!"

Bulk yanked it out of his hand. "He meant to give it to me."

As the three Power Rangers walked back toward the gym, Bulk and Skull were fighting over the mop. "Maybe we should have told them to clean up the science lab, too," Zack joked.

Chapter 29

Inside the gym, a beaming Billy Cranston stood next to his table, where the targeted anti-dimensional energy coherence disrupter had a big blue ribbon stuck on it. The other Power Rangers were there, too, celebrating with their friend. They slapped him on the back, mussed his hair, and made jokes about disrupting his coherence . . .

"Hey, Billy, this is great!" Trini said.

"Well," Billy said. "You did do some of the soldering and the case design and posters. I couldn't have done it without you."

"It was all yours, Billy. You know that." Trini looked around. As the fair wound to a close, experiment teams were breaking down their displays and lugging them back out to their cars. Some of the younger kids were making silly faces in the mirrors left at Bulk and Skull's table.

That was where the whole day started, Trini

thought. *With us pulling into this lot.*

Much had happened since then.

"What did you show them, anyway?" Trini asked Billy. "The judges, I mean."

"I guess I got lucky," he said. "I was able to show them how it worked because I could see Finster's signal right there when I powered it up. I mean, I made this thing in case something like that ever happened, but who would have thought it would happen today?" Billy laughed.

Then he got more serious again. "But I think maybe I overloaded something when I powered it up. Right after . . . well, you know, after everything was all done outside? All the lights in the gym flickered for a second, and then the disruptor burned out. Pop! Just like that."

After a pause, Jason said, "You didn't overload anything, Billy. You're too smart for that. You remember what Lord Zedd said, right?"

They all understood what he meant. Finster and Lord Zedd had struck back. Zedd was sending them a message, just as he had said he would.

All six Power Rangers met in the Command Center so they could make sure Zordon was completely up to date. "Interesting," he said when they had filled him in from all their different angles. "Very interesting. This tells me Lord Zedd doesn't have much support from Rita's former minions. Except Goldar, of course. He will follow whomever he thinks has the most power. But Lord Zedd does not trust them, either. Regardless, we can be certain Lord Zedd will strike again. We have defeated him, and he will nurse his anger until all he can think about is destroying us. We must be ready."

All the Power Rangers nodded. "We will be," Jason said.

"You fought well as a team," Zordon added, "looking out for one another and always having one another's backs. That is why you were victorious today. Remember that."

"We will," Tommy said.

Zordon looked from one Power Ranger to the next, seeing their dedication and their courage. Now that he had told them all the serious things, Zordon had one lighter sentiment to deliver.

"Oh," he said. "And, Billy, congratulations on the science fair."

SABAN'S

MIGHTY MORPHIN

POWER RANGERS

FISH in TROUBLED WATER

Chapter 1

Despite all the flashing lights along the Command Center's computer panels, Billy Cranston, the sandy-haired Blue Ranger, remained completely focused on his work. The wrist-communicators he was trying to adjust were terribly important.

And he should know—he'd invented them!

The communicators not only allowed the five Mighty Morphin Power Rangers to contact one another at any time, but they also linked them to the Command Center's teleporter. That way, they could fight any monstrous attacks from the evil witch Rita Repulsa and her minions on a moment's notice, anywhere on Earth. Without the communicators, they'd have to wait for Zordon's robotic assistant, Alpha 5, to operate the teleporter for them.

Billy's invention had worked reliably until that morning, when a large storm began on the surface of the sun. Solar storms were common, but the flares they produced interfered with everything from radio signals to auto engines to Internet transmissions. Now they prevented the communicators from working. The storm would pass, sooner or later. In the meantime, Billy hoped he could get them up and running, in case there was an emergency.

So far, it wasn't looking good.

Much as his fellow Power Rangers wanted to get back to Angel Grove and enjoy some rare downtime, they knew not to hover while Billy worked. Alpha 5, who looked like a human except for his saucerlike head, was incredibly curious about anything humans did. The robot couldn't keep from asking questions.

"Why are you boosting the frequency instead of checking the circuits, Billy?" Alpha 5 asked.

Billy usually didn't mind. "I checked them before we got here," he answered.

Zordon, their guide and mentor, spoke up. "Alpha 5, let's let Billy concentrate while you work on tracking the solar flares. A solar storm of this magnitude could interfere with the teleporter itself! If he can figure out a way around that, it could be crucial in case of an attack!"

Billy knew the wise sage himself would love to do

more. After all, Zordon had fought Rita Repulsa ten thousand years ago, sealing her and her evil minions in a space Dumpster on the moon. Unfortunately, a last-ditch spell from the wicked witch had trapped Zordon in a time warp. With Rita free again, Zordon had to direct the battle from a special energy tube that maintained his delicate connection to this dimension and allowed him to communicate with the Power Rangers.

The tube also made him look like a big floating head. But his words, and his wisdom, were vital.

Billy's technical wizardry seemed like magic to some, but it was really just science. While he was good at it, there was only so much he could do. After two hours, he was about to call it quits when his phone alarm beeped, reminding him of another important responsibility.

Wiping his hands, he took a plastic bottle labeled FOOD from his pocket and sprinkled a few dried flakes into a small bowl he'd left on the Command Center workbench.

The goldfish inside munched away.

Alpha 5 turned his metal head. "You're taking a break to feed your pet?" he asked.

As he answered, Billy studied the fish. "Goo Fish

Junior isn't just a pet. He's part of an experiment."

Surprised to hear the name he'd given his fish, the other Power Rangers immediately stopped what they were doing. Kimberly Ann Hart, the Pink Ranger, froze in mid stretch and asked the question they were all thinking: "Isn't Goo Fish the name of a monster we fought?"

Billy nodded. "Yes. Specifically, it's the monster Goldar summoned when Rita Repulsa heard about my ichthyophobia."

Kimberly, Jason, and Zack looked at one another, puzzled.

Trini Kwan, the Yellow Ranger, completed the martial arts maneuver she'd been practicing and explained, "Fear of fish."

She was used to translating Billy's bigger words for the others.

Screwing the cap back on the bottle, Billy faced his friends. "It's thanks to that battle that I got over my fear and can work with fish. So Goo Fish Junior seemed appropriate," he said.

Alpha 5 leaned in for a closer look at the bowl. "An experiment?" he asked.

Billy adjusted his glasses and shrugged. "I've been

so focused on the communicators, I forgot to mention that I've been selected to spend a week, starting tomorrow, with thirty other high-school students at the Marine Island Research Center. We'll get to use the best scientific equipment in the world to work on our own special projects."

The others clapped and hooted. Alpha 5 spun happily in a circle.

Zack Taylor, the bighearted Black Ranger, slapped Billy on the shoulder. "Wow! Good for you, man!" he said.

Jason Lee Scott, the Red Ranger and their team leader, asked, "So, what's your experiment?"

Billy grinned proudly. "Using electroencephalography to image the brain waves of *Carassius auratus* for interspecies communication," he announced.

Jason, Zack, and Kimberly nodded. Then they looked to Trini.

"It's a way to get goldfish and people to talk to each other by reading their brain waves," she explained.

"Fantastic!" Kimberly said.

"Hey, that's what Trini does for you!" Zack joked.

Billy laughed along with them. Much as he loved his friends, he had to admit there were times he wished he didn't need any translator.

"I hate to step on your good news, Billy," Jason said, "but is there any hope for the communicators?"

Billy shook his head and began handing back the devices. "I've done everything I can, but until the storm passes, our contact with one another will be bad to none. In 1859 the biggest solar storm on record, called the Carrington Event, peaked for only a few days, so this should pass soon." He looked up at the sage's benevolent face. "Zordon, do you think I should cancel?"

"Your selflessness is appreciated, Billy," Zordon said. "But I'm confident Rita is still licking her wounds from her last battle with the Power Rangers. Your work on fish communication will help advance humanity's connection to the seas, and that is just as important."

Even Jason, who was the most serious about the Rangers, agreed. "I'm sure we can manage for a few days," he said.

"If we had to, we could walk!" Zack added.

Appreciating the support, Billy looked at Goo Fish Junior. "Guess we're going on a trip, little guy. What do you think of that? Hey, maybe soon I can actually ask you, and you'll be able to answer me!"

Goo Fish Junior only bubbled in response.

Chapter 2

In the ancient, multi-towered Moon Palace, 238,900 miles away, Rita Repulsa, the evil witch who wanted to dominate the galaxy, was very angry. She stomped around the workshop set aside for her monster-making minion Finster. Whenever she whirled, her flowing gown and crescent–moon–tipped wand sent alchemical potions, supplies, and notebooks flying. Finster, a short, furry, pointy-eared alien inventor, raced about behind her, catching his tumbling things when he could.

I have to wonder, Finster thought, *if she's doing all this damage on purpose!*

He knew better than to ask, though.

Finster had been loyally serving Rita for ages and still faithfully believed in her evil dreams. Ever since some unwitting astronauts from Earth released them from the cramped space Dumpster Zordon had trapped them in, they'd lived there in the Moon

Palace. There'd been good times and bad—mostly bad, thanks to the Power Rangers.

Today, though, Rita was in a particularly lousy mood.

"I'm sick of it, Finster! Sick of losing!" she shrieked. "I mean, how am I supposed to dominate an entire galaxy if I can't beat five putrid power punks? So what if my worst enemy, Zordon, helps them out? There's not much he can do, trapped in that time warp!"

When Finster didn't answer fast enough, she gave the biggest thing in the workshop, his Monster-Matic, a kick. Finster winced as if he'd been kicked himself. The Monster-Matic was his greatest invention. It allowed him to create everything from the faceless Putty Patrol to all manner of monsters, using his special clay.

Rita had a point, though. To date, they'd all been defeated by the Power Rangers.

Angry, she shook her wand at him and said, "You and this contraption better come up with something new and powerful that will take Zordon's ridiculous Rangers out once and for all!"

Like any good evil queen, Rita tended to be extreme. She was either laughing hysterically or getting enraged. Sometimes it was very hard for

Finster to tell which was coming next. It did keep Finster and her other minions, Goldar, Squatt, and Baboo, on their toes, though.

She waited for a response. Finster knew he had to say *something*, but all the drama left him mumbling.

"Well, your wickedness," he said softly. "I do have this idea I've been working on."

She wheeled toward him so fast that her dual-horned hairdo tipped over and nearly threw her off balance. Crouching like a stalking tigress, she pointed at her ear. "What'd you say? Speak up!"

Finster cleared his throat. "I said, I have an idea."

She rubbed her hands together. "An idea? Is it a new monster? An even bigger monster?" she asked excitedly. "A *monster*-size monster? I like it already!"

"Not exactly, my queen. It's a . . . device," Finster said. Instead of describing a terrifying creature, he held up a small rectangular gadget. It was full of buttons and lights. It looked so harmless, a human might mistake it for a TV remote.

Seeing it, her face dropped.

"I call it the Enhancifier," Finster said hopefully.

She grabbed it and turned it over. Then she made a face.

"The what? The fancy-liar? The pants-on-fire?" she asked.

"Enhancifier, your dreadfulness," he said. "With it, I can take any living creature, meld it with a preselected monster clay, and quintuple its power."

From the puzzled look on her face, Finster realized she didn't know the word.

"It's like double, only . . . more. Err . . . twice more and add one, your malevolence," Finster explained.

She stiffened. "Math?" she asked, insulted. "You want me to do math? Oh, just listening to you is giving me a headache! Baboo makes the gadgets; you stick to your clay!"

She threw the Enhancifier into the air.

Finster gasped then caught it. "But, your nastiness—" he said.

"No!" she said, cutting him off. "I've had enough of your big words and fancy arithmetic! I'm going to take a nap!"

As she stormed off, Finster started moping. Yes, of course his clay and the Monster-Matic were wonderful, but he knew he was also every bit as good with gadgets as that silly cross between a monkey and a bat, Baboo. Pouting, he started to clean up the mess

Rita had made in his workshop.

Why, even Rita herself says she only keeps Baboo around so there'll be someone to blame when something goes wrong! Finster thought. *And I know the Enhancifier is a perfectly good idea. If only I could get her terrible-ness to pay attention long enough to understand!*

Then, as if to prove to himself that he was an excellent inventor, he came up with a new idea.

I've got it! he thought. *I can use the Enhancifier to create something Rita does understand—that new, monstrous monster she wants, a great brute that's certain to squash the Power Rangers. All I need is the right animal. Then she'll see what I mean!*

Determined, Finster tiptoed out of his workshop. After making sure the wicked queen had indeed gone to sleep, he crept onto the observation balcony on the upper floor of the palace. There he found Rita's extreme long-range telescope and aimed it toward the distant blue-green Earth.

"There are so many different kinds of animals down there," he mused. "What sort would impress Rita the most? It has to be large and powerful to begin with, so my Enhancifier can make it even stronger. The humans keep some large animals in zoos, like elephants, but I want something even more spectacular."

And then he saw it, just off the California coast, in the Pacific Ocean: the Marine Island Research Center. It was the perfect place to begin his search.

"Whales, megasharks, giant squids!" he squealed. "There are plenty of powerful, frightening creatures out there!"

The next morning the solar storm had gotten so bad, Zordon warned that, aside from Billy, the others should stick together since the communicators would be ineffective. But the solar flares didn't make the weather in Angel Grove any less sunny and beautiful. His notes and belongings packed, Billy said goodbye to his fellow Power Rangers and boarded a sleek water shuttle for the journey to the research center.

As the shuttle pulled out from the dock, they all waved. Trini called out, "Don't be afraid to make new friends!"

Billy waved back. She was only half kidding. He tended to be quiet around people he didn't know, and his fellow contest winners, from all over the country, would be strangers. But he could worry about that when he got there. In the meantime, the ocean ride was so bumpy, he was plenty busy trying to keep Goo Fish Junior's bowl from spilling over.

Two hours later, when Billy finally stepped off the shuttle and had his first up-close look at the Marine Island Research Center, he realized it was worth being shaken up a little. The research center was bigger than it had seemed in the pictures and even more amazing than he'd imagined.

There was a beautiful mountain at the far end of the island, with freshwater falls and a large, peaceful palm-tree forest. Closer to the docks, there were state-of-the-art buildings where the world's top marine biologists studied the ocean and all its creatures. A plaza had open-air pools for smaller species, but the five-story, 150-foot-tall main building, where Billy and the other students would live and work, had more than ten huge tanks for the bigger specimens.

Not just specimens, Billy reminded himself. The living creatures the scientists studied there were called "guests" and treated that way. They were always returned, unharmed, to their ocean homes. Billy loved the care and respect the scientists showed. He thought even the environmentally conscious Trini would approve.

Carrying the fishbowl and his belongings, Billy followed the welcome signs. As he got closer to the entrance to the main building, he had to stop and marvel. A member of the *Pseudorca crassidens* species, the fourth-largest type of dolphin, was sweeping gracefully along on the other side of a clear Plexiglas wall that formed part of one of the gigantic tanks inside.

Looking down at another fellow "guest," Billy said, "Don't worry, Goo Fish Junior. Big isn't the same as important."

The registration table was just around the curved Plexiglas. Seeing all the teens gathered there, Billy gulped. He hoped they hadn't heard him talking to Goo Fish Junior. Without a proper explanation, that might seem a bit strange, and he wanted to make a good first impression. He wasn't Zack, after all, who could walk into any room, tell a joke, and make friends.

But the students seemed too busy gawking at their new surroundings to have noticed. They weren't very talkative, either. They were probably tired and woozy from their own journeys. Making an effort, Billy smiled and nodded nervously at a few. He tried to think of something to say other than hello. But, smart as he was, he couldn't.

Finally, a thin redheaded boy, who seemed pretty

nervous himself, came closer and squinted at his name tag.

"So . . . Billy," he said. "I'm Ira. What's your project?"

Of course. It was a perfect question. They all had projects. Billy wished he'd thought of it but was just as happy to be asked.

"I'm using electroencephalography to image brain waves of . . . ," he began. Remembering the Power Rangers' befuddled reactions, he stopped himself. "I guess I should probably explain what *electroencephalography* means . . ."

A few of the students who were listening laughed nervously.

"Uh, did I say something wrong?" Billy asked.

Ira coughed a little and said, "No, not really. It's just that I think everyone here *knows* what *electroencephalography* means!"

A cheerful girl came up and pointed at the bowl in Billy's hands. "And does that adorable little *Carassius auratus* have a name?"

Knowing the Latin for goldfish, Billy brightened. "Goo Fish Junior," he said. Taking Ira's cue, he read her name tag. "What's your project, Alani?"

"I'm working on some spacecraft-navigation

software based on the shark's ability to sense the Earth's magnetic field," she said.

A black-haired teen with thick glasses raised his hand to speak, as if he were in a classroom. When they all turned his way, he said, "Hey, I'm Kevin and . . . uh, I know a joke. Why did the chicken cross the Möbius strip? To get to the same side!"

When they all laughed loudly, without anyone having to explain that a Möbius strip only *has* one side, it really broke the ice. Then they all started talking. In fact, Kevin reminded Billy a little of Zack.

Things kept getting better. During orientation, Billy learned that all the scientists working there, including the head of the center, the famous Dr. Anton Fent, would offer advice and guidance, but only if they were asked. He also found out that each student would have their own private lab space to use.

Billy was already feeling pretty great when he found his assigned space. One look at all the equipment made him give off a long, low whistle. "Wow!" he said. "With this, I can do in days what would've taken months, or a year, at Angel Grove High!"

Happily, he unpacked and made sure Goo Fish Junior's feeding schedule was up to date.

But then he heard a dreadful clatter from the hall outside his door. Relaxed as he was, Billy's Power Ranger instincts kicked in. When he opened the door and saw some suspicious shadows shifting in the hall, his first thought was that it was one of Rita Repulsa's monsters, thanks to the overall stench!

Rushing outside, Billy almost exhaled when he saw who was causing the racket.

Almost, but not quite.

It was Farkas "Bulk" Bulkmier and Eugene "Skull" Skullovitch, the two hapless bullies from back home. Dressed in gray overalls, Bulk and Skull were trying to pick up a bucket and mop they'd knocked over. Every time they tried, though, they somehow managed to keep bumping each other.

Billy loudly cleared his throat. "What are you two doing here?" he asked.

Startled, they both nearly fell over. Once they realized it was the "loser" they knew from Angel Grove High School, they straightened and did their best to look tough.

Bulk huffed. "So it's our old pal, Billy Cranston. You're one of the nerd types crawling all over this place, huh? It just so happens that Skull and I have decided to engage in some gainful employment here, as temporary custodial engineers."

Billy shook his head at the illogicality. "You two never cared about work before," he said. "And if you don't like 'nerd types,' why take a job that leaves you stuck with us for a week?"

Skull scrunched his face. "Hey," he said, "we're not stuck here with you. You're stuck here with us!"

Bulk patted his friend on the shoulder. "Exactly! When we heard there'd be as much free food as you can eat and a bunch of losers to push around, we signed right up with our fake IDs! And you'd better not get any ideas about turning us in, or else!"

Once, Billy might have let them push him around. Heck, fish used to scare him! But his experiences as a Power Ranger had given him confidence, even if he couldn't tell them about his other identity.

Billy wasn't used to standing up for himself, especially not to Bulk and Skull, but he held his ground. "Or else what, Bulk?" he asked.

Bulk grinned. "You know."

Billy felt unsure what to do next, but he crossed his arms over his chest. "No, Bulk, I don't," he said. "Why don't you tell me?"

Confused by Billy's confident stance, Bulk fumbled for the right words. "Or else . . . you know. It'll be trouble for you, not the other way around."

Pursing his lips, Skull echoed his partner's words. "Yeah, trouble."

With that, the two strutted off as if they owned the island—but not without nearly tripping again over the bucket and mops they carried.

Relieved his act had worked, Billy realized it could have been worse. *Bulk and Skull are a nuisance,* he thought. *But at least they're not a real threat.*

Chapter 4

As the Blue Ranger returned to his lab, he failed to notice a short alien figure skulking among the shadows farther down the hall. As the figure neared the open area that contained the big tanks, sunlight from the domed glass ceiling shone on his doglike features.

Afraid he might be seen, Finster stepped back into the shadows. The evil minion couldn't care less about all the busy teens and scientists. He was much more interested in the enormous marine specimens. But he was also in a hurry.

Using alchemical magic on the Moon Palace teleporter to get through the solar storm had been easy. Going to Earth without Rita's permission was dangerous, though. If the wicked queen awoke from her nap and found Finster gone before he could prove the value of his Enhancifier by creating his greatest monster ever, she'd be . . . well . . . *unhappy*, to say the least.

Once Finster made it to the collection of enormous tanks, seeing all the monstrous possibilities made him so giddy, his worries disappeared. As he "shopped" around, checking out one marine creature after another, it was all he could do to keep himself from clapping like a child in a toy store.

Now, now, he reminded himself. *I'm a scientist and an inventor. There'll be plenty of time for giddy clapping later. This is a time for clear thinking! My choice has to be perfect!*

The blue whale in the biggest tank caught his eye immediately. Pressing his hands against the thick Plexiglas for a closer look, Finster thought his mission might already be accomplished.

But something made him hesitate.

Is it really the best I can do? he wondered.

True, the whale was enormous. It was, of course, as big as a whale! But there was something too . . . *peaceful* about the giant. It made Finster worry whether it had the heart to attack anyone, let alone the Mighty Morphin Power Rangers.

"This is more like it!" he said, turning to the next tank. "The great white shark is a classic killing machine! Still . . . classic can also be cliché. I want something even more impressive."

Like a picky shopper, he found something wrong with nearly every choice. The giant spined sea star, with its ability to regrow limbs, or the giant spider crab, with its armor-like exoskeleton, were fearsome, but . . . not quite as big as Finster wanted.

The billowing, poisonous tentacles of the lion's mane jellyfish were much more like it!

Or the Portuguese man-of-war!

Or the giant isopod!

Strengthened by his Enhancifier, any one of them could crush the Power Rangers.

Soon he had the opposite problem. There were too *many* great choices.

This will be a tough decision, he thought, chuckling. *A tough decision, indeed!*

Chapter 5

Back in his student lab, a certain teen with attitude had filled Goo Fish Junior's little glass bowl with waterproof sensors, speakers, and microphones. Billy hoped they would not only record the fish's brain waves, but also let Billy "talk back" with sounds, lights, or bubbles, whichever worked best for a goldfish. Color-coded wires led from the bowl, across the worktable and floor to a high-powered computer. From there, they were connected to a fancy headset that Billy wore.

Ready for his first try, Billy leaned in close to the bowl. "Goo Fish Junior, hello!" he said. "Can you hear me?"

As he spoke, the tiny speakers sent waves through the water, a gentle light flashed Morse code, and a little tube gave off a sequence of bubbles.

When Goo Fish Junior seemed to bubble back, Billy got incredibly excited.

Did it work? he wondered. *What will the fish say?*

But the computer only translated: "Blorp, boop, blop."

"Oh well," Billy said to the fish. "At least I proved the equipment works. Once I make some changes to the sensors, I should be able to *see* what you're thinking. Maybe then the computer can create a better version of fish-speak. You probably only want to tell me how crowded it is in there, anyway, huh? This is going to take a little soldering . . ."

No sooner did Billy find the soldering iron than there was a knock at the door.

"Come—" he said.

Before he finished the invitation, a very hurried and very *wet* Ira and Alani charged in. They were followed by a group of other students. Together, they made Billy's lab almost as crowded as the fishbowl.

And it wasn't just Ira and Alani who were wet—everyone was. At first, Billy thought they'd gone swimming, but they seemed upset.

"What's wrong, guys?" he asked.

Ira bent over to shake some of the water from his hair, as he explained, "These two custodial engineers spilled their bucket on us! I'm not even sure they *meant* to do it. They were tripping all over the place, so it could have been an accident. But when I asked them to apologize, they called us losers and said they'd do it again!"

Alani was fuming. "Custodial engineers, ha!" she said. "I don't think they've had any janitorial training at all!"

Randal, a blond boy, looked especially shaken up. He leaned against the doorframe and sadly wrung his shirt dry. "I really hate this," he said. "It's bad enough that I have to deal with bullies back home. How am I going to complete a decent aquatic toxicology study if I'm constantly looking over my shoulder?"

Feeling bad for his new friends, Billy passed around the few towels he'd packed and sighed. "Unfortunately," he said, "I'm very familiar with those two. But trust me, you don't have to worry about them anywhere near as much as you do your own fear. If you stand up to Bulk and Skull, they'll back off. I promise."

Randal twisted his brow as tightly as he had his shirt. "No offense, Billy, but not worrying is easier said than done for some of us. I mean, look at you. You're so sure of yourself, it's hard to believe you were ever *really* afraid of something."

Me? Sure of myself? Billy thought. *I guess being a Power Ranger really has changed me for the better. But that doesn't help them much.*

"I *have* been very afraid," Billy said to Randal. "I've had huge fears, so bad I couldn't move! It started back in grade school. I was trying to create a self-sustaining whirlpool in a lake, but the vortex balance was just a little off."

"That can happen to anyone," Ira offered. "And you used your finger to correct it?"

"Exactly. And when I did," Billy continued, "I guess a fish must have mistaken my finger for a worm. Before I knew what was happening, for lack of a better word . . . *chomp!*"

Billy said it so loudly that everyone jumped a little.

He held up his finger and looked at it. "There's no scar, even a tiny mark, but I still remember that bite as if it happened yesterday. After that, for years, I couldn't bring myself to go in any water where there *might* be fish. I'd go to the beach sometimes, but I'd never swim. I'd even stay at least ten yards from the shoreline. I actually said no to scuba diving with my friends. But then . . ."

Billy paused. They all waited eagerly for him to

finish, but it occurred to him that he couldn't exactly tell them how his goldfish's namesake, the monstrous Goo Fish, had immobilized his fellow Power Rangers. The Blue Ranger was the last member of the team left standing. Billy couldn't let them down; he had to do something, no matter how hard it was.

Finally he said, "My friends needed me, so I had to face my fear and get over it. And now . . ." As everyone watched, without hesitating, he stuck his finger into the goldfish bowl. Goo Fish Junior nibbled at it, but the tiny mouth didn't even tickle. "I've conquered my fear."

His fellow "nerd types" were very impressed.

Ira looked downright inspired. "Billy's right! We should stand up to those bullies together, as a team!"

The others nodded. Billy was going to say something else, but Randal, still in the doorway, glanced outside and gulped.

"It's them!" he shouted. "They're coming this way! We've got to get out of here and hide!"

All at once, the frightened teens raced out.

"Wait!" Billy called. He headed after them, but by the time he reached the door, they'd disappeared down the hall. He saw a grinning Bulk and Skull coming from the other direction. They picked up their pace to chase the students.

But Billy stepped out to block their path. "Hey! I want to talk to you! Those guys are really afraid of you."

The two slowed down to face him. Pleased with himself, Bulk snickered. "Yeah, well, that's the point, isn't it?"

"No, it's not the point of anything," Billy said. Although Trini was able to translate for Billy sometimes, none of the Rangers understood how Bulk and Skull thought. "I want you to back off and leave them alone!" he said.

Billy was so loud and confident, it made them shake. Wondering why he was talking so tough, they peered over Billy's shoulder into the lab.

"Your martial arts pal Jason isn't around anywhere, is he?" Bulk asked.

Seeing that the lab was empty of people, they relaxed.

Noticing the fishbowl, though, Skull's eyes lit up. "Oh! Oh! A fishy!" he said.

As excited as a little boy on his birthday, Skull rushed in. Spotting the food container, he grabbed it and started shaking flakes into the bowl.

Billy turned toward Skull. "Stop that!"

Billy was about to take the food container from Skull, but a swaggering Bulk stepped into his path. Even as a civilian, Billy was sure he could move Bulk if he had to, but his Power Ranger training had taught him that violence was only to be used as a last resort. So even though it meant trying to explain something to Skull, Billy gave it his best shot.

"Overfeeding can hurt goldfish," he said. "They're opportunistic feeders. That means they eat as long as there's food and don't know how to stop."

Skull shook in a few more flakes. "Aw, overeating never bothered Bulk. I don't see why it'd hurt Little Bulky here."

"Little Bulky?" Bulk said, half smiling. "That's sweet. Wait. I don't overeat!"

"Please stop," Billy said.

Bulk sneered and aimed his thumb at the door. "Come on, Skull. We've got a whole island of losers to play with!"

When they left, Billy wanted to follow and find his friends. First, though, he had to scoop all the extra flakes out of the fishbowl. It was a long, difficult process, especially with the sensors getting in the way, but he was responsible for the fish's health.

As he worked, something about the way Goo Fish Junior tilted his body made Billy think he looked disappointed.

"Sorry," Billy said. "It's for your own good."

Once he was finished, Billy searched the halls. When he couldn't find Bulk and Skull, he hoped they'd decided to take a break from acting tough. He did find his fellow students, though. They were all together in the cafeteria.

Ira, Alani, and the others had pushed several tables together in the center of the space so everyone would fit. They were having what looked like a very serious meeting. A pile of chemical supplies had been stacked on the floor near their chairs.

Seeing Billy enter, Ira started a round of applause.

Billy half smiled, half frowned. "Thanks," he said, "but . . . what's going on? What's all that stuff?"

As he got closer, he realized that the students had gathered the standard chemical ingredients for stink bombs and flash firecrackers. They'd already made two large buckets of what looked like a powerful liquid glue.

An eager Alani bounced up from her seat. "We're

taking your advice!" she said proudly. "We're going to face our fear of those two bullies and get some payback!"

Billy shook his head. "Wait, no! That's *not* what I meant. If you try to get revenge, you're just stooping to their level."

"Oh no, not at all," Randal said. He pointed at the supplies. "What we've got planned is *much* more sophisticated than anything Bulk and Skull could come up with. Clearly, we are *way* above their level."

"That's not what I meant," Billy said. "You're just becoming bullies yourselves!"

Ira frowned. "But isn't that okay, if you only bully bullies?" he asked.

"No," Billy said. "It isn't."

"Why not?" Alani asked.

Trying to figure out how best to explain, Billy looked off to gather his thoughts. When he did, he saw something very strange in the distance, over by the marine specimen tanks. It was a short, furry figure, clapping happily. At first Billy thought it was Bulk or Skull, but as he narrowed his eyes, the pointy dog ears he saw were unmistakable.

It was Finster!

Without another thought, Billy ran from the cafeteria.

"Sorry!" he called back to the others. "I have to go check on something extremely important. We'll talk later, but please, don't make any more plans until we do!"

Once he was sure that the students couldn't see him, Billy pulled out his Power Morpher and yelled, "It's Morphin Time!"

To be continued...

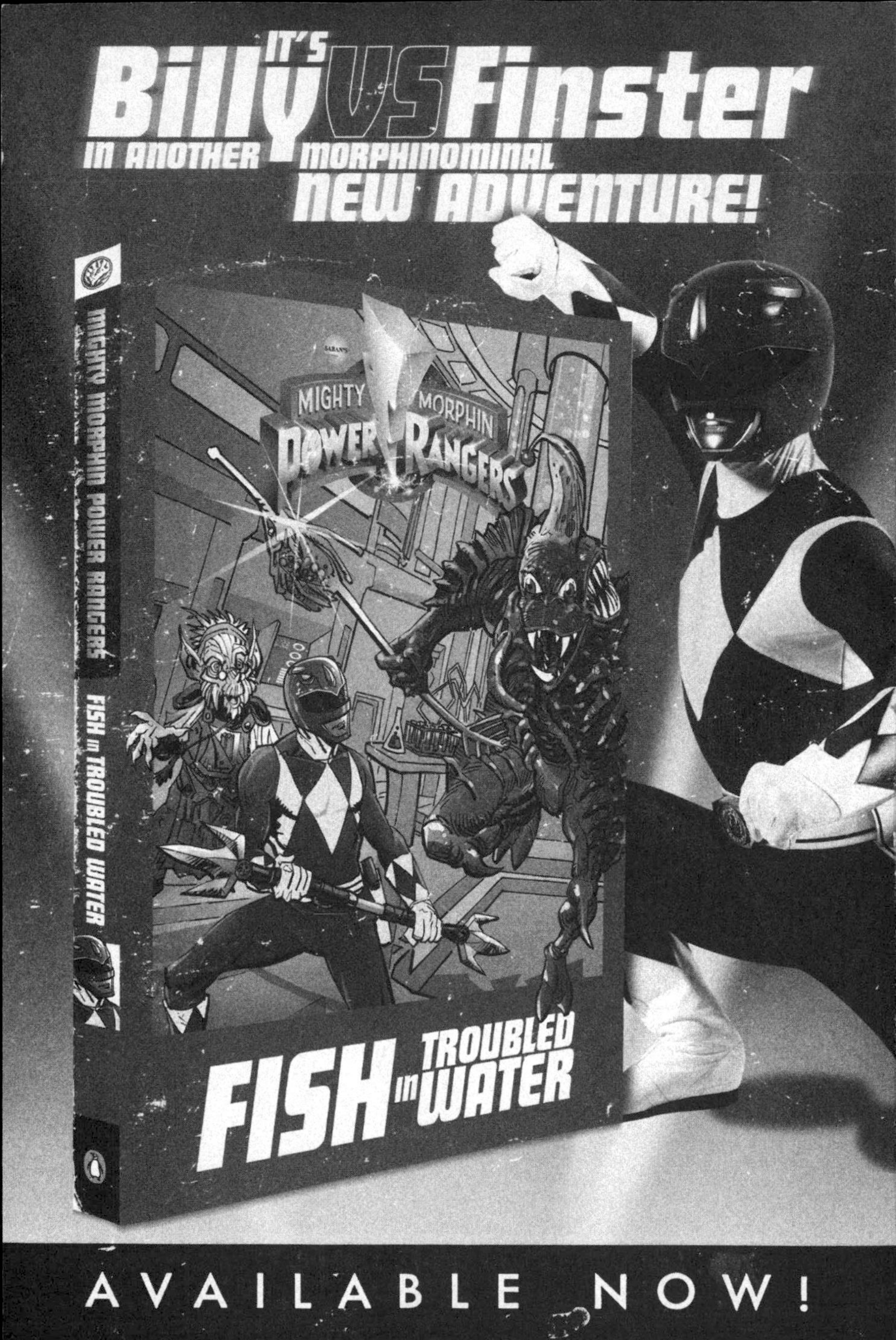
IT'S
Billy VS Finster
IN ANOTHER MORPHINOMINAL
NEW ADVENTURE!
MIGHTY MORPHIN POWER RANGERS
FISH in TROUBLED WATER
MIGHTY MORPHIN POWER RANGERS
FISH in TROUBLED WATER
AVAILABLE NOW!